Qu(

Paul Quatorze

ISBN: 978-1-6876-8476-9

Quoi ?

Quoi?

A novel

Contents :

1 … SATURDAY

Just imagine … I had to walk through the departure lounge at Heathrow Airport with a large wallet thing hanging round my neck. I was following two tiny children, both wearing labels like me. It was totally humiliating.

It was my first proper trip away on my own and we'd had a real row. They'll say it was my fault, but Dad was being quite unreasonable. OK, I'd never flown alone before, but I am almost fourteen. Dad insisted on getting the airline to look after me, like the little ones. He even had to pay extra.

At least we were put on the aircraft first, ahead of the crowd. I had hoped to be able to stow my racquets safely in the overhead lockers but they'd been taken away as potentially dangerous weapons! I had a window seat and wondered if Mum and Dad had gone up to the spectators' roof. Even if they were there, they wouldn't be able to see me. But they could check that we didn't crash on take-off.

I hated the thing round my neck and pushed it down inside my sweater. On aircraft they sometimes give out toys for small children; I prayed they wouldn't offer me anything.

I was looking in the pocket in front of me, safety card, magazine, sick-bag, when someone sat down next to me, heavily.

'Bonjour,' he said, smiling.

'Bonjour,' I replied. I felt good speaking French but it didn't last long.

'Tu voyages seul, sans tes parents ?'

'Er ... excuse me, pardon, quoi?'

'Ah, j'ai pensé que tu parlais français. I am sorry. When you say 'bonjour', I think you speak French.'

'No, we do French at school, but it's not exactly my best subject.'

He grinned. 'Perhaps you are a scientist like me?'

'I don't think the teachers would say I'm an anything,' I replied, 'except perhaps a tennis nut.'

'A tennis nut? Une noix de coco? Like a coconut?'

'No, sorry, we just say nut when someone is hooked on some activity.'

'Ouf, hooked ... your English is difficult for me but it's OK, entendu, I get it.'

He was fumbling to get something out of his jacket pocket. It was a thick tweedy sort of jacket; he must have been boiling hot.

'I also enjoy to play tennis but maybe not as a nut. Here ... please, my card.'

He handed me a business card with his name and address on.

"Vicomte Jean-Marie de Launay de St.Etienne." Underneath there was a string of letters, like people put when they have lots of qualifications. Then there was an address, just Château de somewhere, and a town. No street name or number in the street. There was a string of telephone numbers, for résidence, bureau and portable. He seemed to be very important. Why was he sitting next to me? There were more expensive seats in business class.

'I'm Paul, je m'appelle Paul.'

'Très bien.' We shook hands.

'If we play tennis, you will win. When I was young, I was good, but now I am old.'

Although it was mid-summer, he looked dressed for winter. Cord trousers, a thick check shirt and a wool tie went with the jacket. He had a large bushy beard which made him look even hotter. I had on a T-shirt and cotton chinos. I would have taken my sweater off, except it was hiding the silly label.

'You are going to Geneva?' he asked.

Before I could reply, he went on: 'but that is a stupid question. The aircraft goes to Geneva,
so we must go there all. But after?'

'My uncle's coming to meet me. He lives in Switzerland. He's taking me to a tennis centre for coaching.'

'Alors, il faut que tu parles en français … then you must speak French?'

'No. It's a bit complicated. The centre's in Italy and the coach is German. But I know him already; he speaks English.'

'Ah, mais oui, ça c'est vraiment compliqué.'

He was friendly but I didn't want to have to talk to him for the whole flight so I pulled my phone out of my pocket.

He laughed : 'all young people, everywhere, they have their portables.' He said 'portables' with a French accent and took his own phone out from his brief-case. 'But', he laughed again, 'not only young people!' His phone looked much more modern than mine.

'In England you say mobiles I think but aux Etats-Unis they say cellphones.'

I remembered that Dad had insisted on buying me a French phrase book at WH Smith's at the airport. 'You never know, it might be very useful,' he'd said. Mum had turned over a few pages.

'Yes, dear, look : please can you direct me to the nearest florist's shop. S'il vous plaît, pouvez-vous me dire où se trouve la boutique de fleuriste la plus proche.'

'Mm, I shall probably want to buy lots of flowers,' I laughed.

I started to leaf through the pages. It might be handy because I could use the same question for other shops, other things, but I would need to know the French for the other things.

'You want to read; you must not permit me to talk. But did you understand my card?'

'Yes, I think so, but I don't know what sort of scientist you are; I've no idea what all those letters mean.'

'Bon. I hope you ask. They mean nothing. It is ... how you say ... une blague.

'It is a joke. Many people are very excited, but the letters are nothing.' He laughed loudly. Because he was such a big man, the seat shook. I was a bit embarrassed.

'So what sort of scientist are you?'

'Anything. Everything! You read and I show you later.'

I went back to the phrase-book, but kept glancing at him out of the corner of my eye. He pulled out a notebook from an inside pocket and started to write.

They were pushing the aircraft back from the stand; the usual voice was welcoming us to Swiss International Airlines in several languages. I could pick up a few of the French bits.

'Mesdames et Messieurs,' ... then where you had to put your 'bagages à main', 'le vol est non-fumeur' and what to do with your electronic kit. But it wasn't too hard because they then immediately said the same things in English, about carry-on bags and no smoking.

I always like the take-off. You scream down the runway and then climb really steeply. I like watching the cars and trucks get smaller and smaller.

My neighbour didn't talk again until we were given our snack lunch. He got his first, something special. He turned to me to explain why it was different.

'Je ne suis pas vraiment végétarien, mais je n'aime pas ce repas ... mais non, excuse-moi ... you don't understand!'

'Well, I think I did. You said you're a vegetarian and that's why you've got that food.'

'Bad luck. Almost right. I have said I am not a true vegetarian, but I don't like sometimes the snack. So I command this.'

'You order it,' I said correcting his English, then I quickly apologised: 'I'm sorry, that's very rude!'

'Mais non, c'est bon, we learn only from correction. We say "commander" but you do not command food. You order.'

We talked about tennis. I told him that I had had a lot of coaching and won some junior tournaments. My Dad had fixed extra tuition at a tennis camp where Hans worked in the summer. I'd already had coaching from him in England. Uncle Joe had offered to act as chauffeur.

My new friend laughed.

'Voilà, you speak French. Your "chauffeur".'

It took me a moment or two before I knew what he was talking about. I hadn't even realised that it's a French word.

When we'd both demolished the lunches, I asked him to explain about his science, like he'd promised. He piled my plastic tray on top of his. Then he put his note-book on my tray-table.

'What is this?' he asked, pointing to the open page. There was an untidy drawing of the bottom of a leg, a foot in a boot, and wheels.

'It looks like a roller skate,' I said, 'or ... no ... a blade.'

'Right, you call them I think roller blades. Sometimes also people say in-line skates. Now, it is a bad drawing, but what is different?'

I looked again.

'I'm sorry, I don't know.'

'The wheels. The first wheel and the last wheel, they touch the ground. The others not.'

I had noticed but I'd thought it was his bad drawing.

'Right, but why?'

'I make a new design. Like skis, the new types are a different shape, it is more easy to make the bends, the corners. My skates will be very flexible; we use new material, very secret. When you go straight you go faster. In the corner, the skate flexes, all the wheels are used.'

'It seems brilliant. When will they be available?'

'Ouf, maybe never. First we complete the design, then we try to get the patent, then perhaps ... but remember, this is secret!' I liked the word 'ouf' and decided that could be the start of my real French vocabulary.

He pulled out a large pocket watch; I hadn't noticed before that he was wearing a waistcoat as well as the jacket. Why didn't he die of over-heating?

'Now, please excuse me, I must sleep. If you wish, you may continue to study the design!' He laughed loudly again, then he closed his eyes. I was puzzled by his design idea. How could the blade flex unless your feet flex in the middle too. I couldn't resist turning over the pages to see what else was in his note-book. Quite a long list of words had "minä rakastan sinua" and "szeretlek". I had no idea how to pronounce the second one but, for some reason, "minä rakastan sinua" stuck in my mind.

There were sketches for some sort of drone and notes about water-pumps. Suddenly I realised he was looking at me out of the corner of his eye. I blushed furiously.

'Ça va, ça marche, it's OK. I expected you to look some more.'

'Why are you interested in water-pumps? They are not new.'

'Ils deviennent plus utiles ... global warming. En Suisse nous avons des panneaux solaires, you use the same words, solar panels, also wind-pumps. De temps en temps, from time to time, they will produce much electricity which we can not use immediately. Et nos glaciers diminuent, deviennent plus petits, chaque année. Compris?'

I nodded : 'So you need to store electricity?'

'Exactement! We use electricity to pump water to reservoirs at the top of our mountains and later the water is let to descend to create new electricity ... hydro-electric power.'

'Wow, easy.'

'Il est important que les pompes sont aussi efficaces que possible, more efficient, n'est-ce pas? Now I must rest.'

I went on thinking about the variety of his work, it must be great to have so many different ideas to work on.

My neighbour didn't stir again until the announcement, when they tell you it's the final approach, and ask you to put your seat backs upright.

'Mesdames et Messieurs, nous avons commencé notre descente vers l'aéroport de Genève' ... 'Ladies and gentlemen, we have started our descent to Geneva airport. Please ensure your seat belts are fastened.'

You have to fold up the tray-tables too, so I offered him his note-book.

He looked at me: 'Bonjour, good morning, no ... good afternoon.' He laughed.

I struggled: 'Bon après-midi!'

'Bravo, fantastique, mon ami,' he cried.

I'd been to Geneva once before with Mum and Dad and Richard and Sophie; we'd stayed one night with Uncle Joe on our way for a ski holiday. The aircraft comes down over the lake and the views are brilliant.

'Voilà, la montagne la plus haute d'Europe,' said le Comte. 'It is the highest ...'

'Oh dear,' I thought, 'can I be rude again?' Perhaps.

'Ouf', I said, thinking that would be a good start. 'Actually ...'

'Ah, I know what you will say. Notre Mont-Blanc n'est pas le plus haut. It is only highest in our Alps. I forget, you must tell me ...'

We had done mountains in geography last year and I happened to remember.

'It's in the Caucasus, it's called Elbrus but I'm not sure if I've pronounced it right.'

'Mais oui, ... oui, oui. Elbrus ... en Russe.'

We touched down gently but the runway seemed very bumpy.

As the Airbus slowed to a stop at the arrival gate, he was looking past me out of the window.

'Comme d'habitude. Always it is the same. For this flight they use the gate which is furthest from the terminal.'

'Can I help you?' I offered.

'No, you will be more rapid alone. Your uncle is meeting you?'

'Yes, thanks. It was good to meet you. Some time I would like to hear more about your work.'

'You are very polite. But you have my numéro de téléphone, n'est-ce pas? If you have some time when you return to Geneva, you must take contact.'

I almost corrected him, but managed to stop myself in time. He let me push past him to get out and I grabbed my kit from the overhead locker and left him sorting his own things.

'Au revoir, et je te souhaite de bons matches de tennis!' he said.

'Au revoir, merci!'

When I glanced back over my shoulder, he was still in a muddle and holding up all the people behind him. At the front of the aircraft, the little ones, with labels on, were waiting for me.

'Where is your wallet?' asked the Swiss Airlines lady.

I pulled it out from my sweater.

'It is not permitted to hide it,' she said fiercely. 'We must be able to recognise you.'

On the way to the passport control, she asked who was meeting me. I explained.

'Good, so we shall go to find him and then you can come to get your baggage.'

Uncle Joe is big, very big. When he shakes your hand, he makes it feel like an endangered species. Then he goes for the big arm round the shoulders hug, which is a real crusher.

'Good flight?'

'Yes, great, thanks,' I replied, trying to get some air into my lungs.

The lady told him that we should follow her back into the luggage hall.

Uncle Joe got one of the baggage trolleys and I put my carry-on bag on the top.

As he came back, he said: 'Look over there. Can you see the man with a beard? He's got a chauffeur with him.'

I looked; it was my new friend. Before I could explain, Uncle Joe went on.

'Vicomte de Launay de St. Etienne. He's a banker and lots of other things, one of the richest men in Europe. He lives on the lake here, but not in Switzerland; he's just over the border in France.'

'Yes, I know, he's a friend of mine,' I said laughing.

'What? How? Come on, explain!'

I fished in my pocket for the Vicomte's card. I showed it to Uncle Joe.

'That is seriously impressive. He's a bit of a recluse. He never ever talks to journalists, so nobody really knows the truth about him. There are all sorts of rumours.'

I started to ask how he had become so rich but my bag appeared rolling down the belt. I grabbed it and put it on the trolley.

'La Disco est dans le parking, au sous-sol.'

'Oh, no, Uncle, not yet. I agreed to try some French but later, please.'

'OK, but did you understand?'

'Something about going to a disco?'

'You poor boy, your memory has gone, totally and completely. What do I drive?'

'Ugh, sorry. A Land Rover Discovery, of course. But you usually call him George.'

'Right. George is in the underground car park.'

Uncle Joe pushed a few francs into the car park machine and got his exit ticket. We went down in the lift and loaded the car.

'We'll stay at my place tonight and go on tomorrow. By the way, don't let me forget the bikes. There's room in here to take them.'

'Yea. Great!'

'What's the French for bike?' he asked.

'Bicyclette?' I tried.

'Correct,' he said, laughing, 'until about thirty years ago! These days they are always vélos. They often talk about VTT which means vélo tout terrain ... do you get it? ... all terrain, for mountain bikes.'

We cruised out on to the autoroute, heading for Lausanne. I love driving in the Discovery; you are so high up off the ground.

'I need some gas, so we must stop soon.'

'I assume you mean petrol, or is it diesel?' I replied.

'No, it's the 3.5 petrol engine, which is much quicker, but drinks petrol like mad.'

We soon pulled into a service area. I helped with filling up and then followed Uncle Joe into the shop.

'Grab a drink or an ice,' he said.

'Thanks, what about you?'

'Non, merci.'

He paid with a credit card, then turned to me. 'What's the French for eighty?'

I didn't hesitate for long. 'Quatre-vingts?' I said, a bit questioningly.

'Did you hear what that chap said?'

I had to admit I hadn't been concentrating.

'He said 'huitante-trois total, s'il vous plaît.'

'Quoi?'

'In Geneva they still mainly use proper French, but once you get into the French-speaking part of Switzerland, it changes. Seventy, eighty, ninety is septante, huitante, nonante. Plus facile, n'est-ce pas?'

'That's brilliant. Things like soixante et onze for seventy-one are just horrid. But I bet, if I try using your ones at school, our French teacher will give me a hard time.'

We turned off the motorway near Vevey. Uncle Joe has a super single storey house, with a great view of the lake.

'Let's have a drink. What do you want? Another Coke?'

'Yes, thanks, I haven't changed and it doesn't have to be light or zero.'

'Go out in the garden; I'll bring them out.'

He soon followed me, with a beer for himself, and a big bowl of crisps.

'Voilà, Monsieur, un coca!'

We sat in the sun. The mountains across the lake were quite hazy; Uncle Joe said it was a good sign for the weather. The crisps were the super paprika ones and, after only the airline snack on the plane, I was hungry. I tried not to wolf down the whole bowl.

'Qu'est-ce que tu veux manger ce soir? Pizza, burger or real food?'

'Ouf, I don't mind but I am quite hungry.'

'Ça m'est égal … that's a nice French expression. Egal is like equal. Ça m'est égal … I don't mind, it's all the same to me.

'I'm not cooking so I though we'd go up to Blonay. There's a nice Italian place with pizza, pasta but meat and fish too.'

I was relieved that, apparently, he wasn't going to give me a French lesson all evening.

'Sounds great.'

At the restaurant all the staff seemed to know Uncle Joe and all the usual shaking of hands had to include me. It was still nice and warm and so we sat outside.

'Alors, encore une fois, qu'est-ce que tu veux manger?'

There were pages of Italian and a page of chef's recommendations.

'Tu aimes le poisson? Fish is OK for you? Because I recommend the filets de perche. In England nobody ever eats perch but here they're very popular. They come from the lake. And you get lots of small fillets and a great heap of frites. And a salad first.'

I closed up the menu and said 'Sounds super!' He ordered the same for both of us and persuaded me, without much difficulty, to try the local white wine.

'So,' he said, 'tell me about your new friend, le Vicomte!'

I told him we hadn't talked that much, although I did mention the roller-blade idea and said I'd sneaked a look though his note-book.

'But it's secret; we're not allowed to discuss it. Any way, you must tell me more about him.'

'As I said, nobody knows much. He seems to have inherited some money; they are a very old and famous French family. One of his ancestors was guillotined in the French Revolution.

'He's been a big investor in lots of successful businesses and he does seem to have invented things. But he's so secretive that he sometimes uses other names. If you believe all they put in the papers, he probably invented everything from the wheel to the internet.'

We both had something called Coupe Denmark which was vanilla ice with loads of hot chocolate sauce and lashings of whipped cream. Why Denmark Uncle Joe didn't know but it's now on my list of go-to places!

2 ... SUNDAY

My bedroom had its own bathroom. After what didn't feel like a long sleep I got up and had a shower and then went to find Uncle Joe outside reading his Financial Times.

'Good afternoon,' he said.

'Sorry Uncle, that means I'm late. Why didn't you call me?'

'I guessed you would have forgotten about the clocks; il y a une heure de différence entre l'Angleterre et la Suisse. And don't keep calling me uncle; it makes me feel bloody old.'

'No, I had changed my watch but I didn't know what time you'd want to leave.'

'When I'm on my own,' he told me at breakfast, 'I often just have coffee and chocolate biscuits, usually digestive or, if I can get them, dark chocolate HobNobs, they're the best.'

I bet lots of adults would do that if they didn't have children around, but how many would admit it? Today Joe had got some pains au chocolat specially; they were brilliant. I washed them down with Coke; he pretended to throw up.

Mum seems not very keen on him. He's Dad's older brother and he's already been more or less retired for two or three years, though he can't be much more than fifty. I reckon Mum thinks Dad is a bit envious of Uncle Joe. Because he hasn't got a wife and three children, he's much better off than we are. I think Mum's wrong. Dad wouldn't exchange me and Richard and Sophie, trade us in for a stack more money and a house in Switzerland, would he?

We loaded up the Discovery and drove back up to the motorway.

'C'est bon que j'habite si près de l'autoroute.' He had already insisted that we try to have our conversations in French.

'Et aussi proche à La Veyre.' He pointed to some buildings with roofs covered in solar panels.

'OK, I think I've got that : you live near the motorway and La Veyre, that's your tennis club?'

'Bien joué, well done. Perhaps we can have a game there when we get back. Damn, that should have been in French.'

'OK, let me try. On peut jouer là ... when we return. Quand nous revenons?'

'Oui, oui, ou on peut dire "jouer là à notre retour".'

The journey was a mixture of motorways and mountains. On the first part, Joe pointed out a spectacular railway bridge, high over a rocky gorge.

'They do bungee jumping from there. Quite mad! You pay a hundred francs or more to jump off into space. What's the fun in that?'

'I suppose it shows you've got bottle,' I reply.

'Well, I certainly haven't then.,' he laughed. 'And I don't think we'd say bouteille ... I guess it would be je n'ai pas le courage pour ça!'

'Which sort of reminds me ... did you hear about the cannibal who went on holiday,' I asked him, 'and came back with only one leg?'

'No,' he said, 'tell me.'

'It was a self-catering holiday!'

He laughed much more loudly this time.

'And in French?'

'Ouf', I replied. 'Aucune idée! I don't know the words for cannibal and self-catering.'

'That's easy and difficult. Cannibal is the same in French but for self-catering they use the word gîte and the joke doesn't work so well with that.'

'What about the man who went into the pet-shop...'

'En français,' said Joe firmly.

'Ouf, OK, il y avait un monsieur, il a entré ... what's a pet-shop?'

15

'Facile … une boutique d'animaux … continue!'

'OK, ce monsieur est entré dans une boutique d'animaux. Et il a demandé … damn, what's wasp … and what's to buy?'

'Une guêpe et acheter.' Joe looked puzzled.

'Il a dit je veux acheter une guêpe. The salesman, manager … and sell?'

'Le vendeur, le patron … et vendre …' This time he laughed.

'Il a répondu : mes excuses, monsieur, mais nous ne vendons pas les guêpes. Ouf, alors, pourquoi vous avez une guêpe dans la fenêtre?'

Joe had guessed the punch-line and still had to correct me : 'a shop-window is une vitrine, not une fenêtre, but it's a good story and you'll be able to tell it in French when we get there.'

'But we don't know yet, the others may all be Italian or German.'

'Eh bien, je pense qu'il y aura certainement une jeune-fille française là-bas.'

So there would be a French girl but I wondered how Joe knew. Before I could ask him …

'Je vais prendre le col du Grand Saint-Bernard, d'où viennent les chiens.'

'What. Sorry, quoi?'

'You know, dogs with barrels of brandy round their necks to rescue frozen travellers. If some poor guy got lost in a blizzard, he'd have to hope a dog would turn up and give him a tot of brandy.'

'Doesn't sound very likely to me,' I said.

There were big fluffy soft toy ones outside several shops and cafés.

'I think the truth is that they did have rescue dogs long ago, operating from the monastery up the top here, but the barrels were a more recent marketing idea. And there is a story that one dog rescued forty people but was shot by the forty-first chap, because he thought it was a wolf.'

'Joe, you're a mine of really useful information,' I laughed.

At one point, we drove past a small lake. Even though it was early summer, there were chunks of ice like mini-icebergs. Around the lake were several fishermen.

'They must be mad,' I said. 'Surely they won't catch anything if the water's that cold.'

'Ah mais oui,' replied Joe. 'Ils attrapent les poissons prêts à être surgelés, ready-frozen! They can put their catch straight in the freezer, the congélateur!'

I looked at him. He had a totally straight face.

'You have to be, yes, you are joking.'

He giggled happily.

'But I had you for a moment; you weren't sure!'

'Yea, yea, of course I'd believe you if you said they catch fish fingers for Bird's Eye!'

'We're getting near the top. We don't go over the pass any more; they've built a tunnel through the mountain to keep the road open longer in winter. And the frontier into Italy is at the tunnel. I can't remember which end but we may need passports.'

'OK, they're both here, in the glove box.'

In fact they just waved us straight through.

At a motorway service place after we'd crossed into Italy, we stopped for a snacky sort of lunch, more unhealthy food. They had an odd system that you had to decide what you wanted, go and pay for it, then come back to collect it. Don't they trust us?

The last part of the drive was good, except for one thing. I had to navigate. Finding my way with the aid of a map is not one of the skills at which I am even slightly above average. Why didn't Joe have GPS, satellite navigation?

'I'll probably have to have it on the next one I buy, but I know where I'm going!'

'So why do I have to map-read?'

'It's good for you. Don't argue … et en français! Eh bien, vite, il faut te décider, à droite ou à gauche?'

'Quoi?'

Luckily I recognised right and left.

'A gauche, er, I think, je crois.'

He stopped in a lay-by.

'Peut-être, c'est meilleur, si ... don't you think?'

He grabbed the book.

We'd found out about the tennis place through the German coach. He works at a club in London, where I've had coaching, but comes out to Italy to help during the summer holidays. He'd offered me some free coaching. Dad told Uncle Joe all about it and he'd said he'd be happy to drive me there.

'Ouf, c'est facile. Look, it's easy.' He pointed out the route.

'Yes, OK, facile for you. You know where we are! Vous savez où nous sommes.'

'Bien … but you should say tu to me, not vous. Tu sais où nous sommes'.

'I thought it's polite to say vous to old people!'

He tried to smack me but I dodged.

'Please drive carefully … Uncle!'

A couple of kilometres later there was a scruffy sign, with paint peeling off; it showed the name of our hotel with an arrow.

'Très élégant,' said Joe.

The girl who checked us in to the hotel gave us two keys and pointed upstairs.

'Grazie.' I don't think Joe's Italian is quite as good as his French, but it was sure to be better than her English.

The rooms were tiny but we each had our own bathroom with a shower. Mine didn't have a toilet, but I decided that wasn't too important. If I was desperate during the night, I could always use the shower!

We went to have a look round. There was a big pool with several people lying in the sun. On one sun-bed, beer in hand, lay Hans, our tennis coach. He leapt up, spilling beer on the yellow mattress.

'Paul, great, you made it. Welcome to our tennis centre, home for the Centre Court stars of tomorrow!'

There was a lot of shaking hands. I introduced Uncle Joe; Hans pointed to a blonde lady lying on the next sun-bed.

'This is my friend Ilse. She may prefer not to stand up.'

Ilse waved a hand. She was lying face down, wearing half a bikini. There was no sign of the top half. Like Hans, Ilse's name sounds German; I wondered if she spoke English.

'This is our little siesta,' he went on, 'afternoon tennis starts at four o'clock. You've had some lunch?'

We said yes and I promised to be on court at four o'clock.

'You'd better go and sort out your gear,' suggested Joe. 'I'll see you later.'

Mum swears I'm the most untidy person in the world. Once I'm away from home, and on my own, I'm really quite organised. If Mum never picked things up for me, or put anything away, then I would develop my own sort of tidiness. I know where everything is, at least till she puts it somewhere else.

All my tennis kit was beautifully ironed, although I always tell Mum not to bother. She had packed at least three of everything and even more socks and pants. I stuffed it all into a couple of drawers except for what I was about to put on. I was more careful with the rest of the things, shirts for the evenings and some smarter trousers.

I chose new kit for this first session on court; it might be important to make a good first impression. When I'd asked Hans on the telephone how many of us there'd be, he'd had no idea.

'We get lots of last moment reservations, when people can't find anywhere better to go,' he'd joked. At least I hoped it was a joke.

I haven't stayed in many hotels but this was certainly not the smartest ever. I stood in the middle of the room and, stretching my fingers, I could touch both walls at the same time. I wondered if it had been converted from a passage.

I looked at my watch. Almost four already. I never get ready for things till the last moment. I threw on my clothes, checked my hair and added the Nike cap. I grabbed my rather oversize bag and ran down the stairs. There were three courts in a line all with the loose clay surface that they normally use abroad, like the French Open at Roland Garros … and Rome and Madrid and lots of others. There was one more separate hard court probably for bad weather or the winter.

'Ah, Mr. Nike, almost on time, making a big entrance to impress the ladies!'

I blushed. It is so embarrassing to go bright red whenever someone draws attention to me but I can't help it.

'Now we can complete the introductions. Mr. Nike's first name is Paul.'

There were only three others plus Hans on the court. He waved at me.

'Paul, come and shake some hands.'

'Caroline, voici Paul.'

He pronounced her name and mine the French way. We shook hands.

'Elle vient de Paris. En Angleterre ta mère m'a dit que tu parles un peu français,' Hans went on.

'OK, she's from Paris, but what else?' I asked.

'Come on, you can understand that; I said your mother has told me at home that you do speak some French.'

'Very little and only if … you … speak … very … slowly.'

'Seulement … si … tu … parles … très … lentement!' said Caroline laughing.

'I shall try to speak English,' she went on, quite slowly; 'but it is necessary that you try to speak French. Perhaps we teach other.'

I was still blushing, but she was smiling and trying to help, so I smiled back.

'OK, we'll try.'

'No,' she said at once; 'say: d'accord, nous essayerons!'

'D'accord, nous l'essayons' I grinned. 'But you say OK in French, as well!'

'OK, d'accord,' she agreed.

'When you two have finished, we are here to learn tennis, not languages,' said Hans.

'This is Claudia, who comes from Bonn.   Her father is American, so she speaks a little English.'

'Hi!' She waved a hand at me, then scowled at Hans: 'I can correct your English any day you like!'

'And this ...', he waved at the other boy, 'is Luc. Il vient aussi de Paris. Il ... vient ... aussi ... de ... Paris!'

'... et ... je ... ne ... parle ... pas ... anglais,' said Luc.

'Of course that is not true,' said Hans, 'but for everyone's benefit, we shall speak two languages on court, French and English. Claudia and I will be polite; we shall only speak German when we want to have private jokes about the rest of you!'

They seemed a reasonable group. Caroline must be about my age, maybe a bit older.   She was quite tall and very slim. She had very short hair, almost a crew cut.   She was wearing a white T-shirt and shorts, not a skirt. Although they were plain, I was quite sure they had some designer labels somewhere.

Claudia was a bit younger but behaved as grown-up as possible.   She obviously reckoned she was much more American than German.   She had the most enormous tooth braces I'd ever seen.   Some girls manage to look as though they've got used to them. Claudia didn't!

I knew immediately that I wasn't going to get on well with Luc. The way he talked, walked, even looked at me while I was talking, worried me. He was going to want to win everything. Not just any and every game, but every point, and probably every conversation. OK, I'm competitive too, but ...

'Alors, pour commencer, I want you to hit balls as though you are going to play a doubles match,' said Hans.

'Paul, you partner Claudia, Caroline et Luc, l'équipe de France ... the French team. You can speak to your partners in your own language.'

This seemed a good idea, but I wished I spoke French. I'd have much preferred to be paired with Caroline.

Hans climbed up and sat on the umpire's chair.

We just hit balls for a while. Luc and I both took the backhand courts so we were not hitting against each other. Everything I hit towards Caroline she returned with a vengeance.

'OK,' said Hans, 'on peut commencer, let us begin.'

He took us through a routine of shots, forehand and backhand, ground strokes and volleys, checking our skills. Half way through, we were separated on to two courts to practise some more, singles instead of doubles. I was now opposite Luc. Finally, after showing Hans how we could serve, he told us to play a few games.

'Tu peux commencer,' said Luc. I knew he was telling me to serve first, but I pretended not to understand.

'What? ... er ... quoi?'

'Tu ... you ...,' and he signalled for me to serve.

First serve, into the net. The second much better, wide and curling away from his outstretched fore-hand.

'Faute,' he cried.

I knew it wasn't out, but something made me decide not to argue yet. I served again, this time to the backhand court, the first one into the net.

'Chuck it higher,' I said to myself.

He ran round my second serve and put it straight back down the line, a good shot.

'Zéro trente,' he shouted.

He strutted across to the forehand side. He was beginning to annoy me quite a lot.

He won that game to fifteen then took the next to love. I knew I was better than him; I was letting him get to me. Hans and Uncle Joe had come over to watch.

After five games, he was winning four one. By then there had been two more dodgy line calls from his end but I'd kept quiet.

'OK, ça suffit pour aujourd'hui; that's enough for today,' said Hans. 'On court in the morning at nine. Neuf heures du matin.'

Joe started to ask if I was enjoying myself. Luc was talking to Hans, loudly. We both overheard what he was saying.

'J'espère qu'il y aurait d'autres personnes pour l'entraînement. Je ne veux pas jouer toujours avec cet Anglais.'

'What did he say?' I asked Uncle Joe.

'Oh, he was just asking if there were going to be more people training.'

'And ...?' I knew he'd been talking about me, something about anglais.

'Well, I think he was implying that he didn't want to play only with you.'

'He's a prick and a cheat,' I said angrily.

'Hey, you've barely met him.'

'Uncle Joe, I have played a lot of tennis, a hell of a lot. Every so often, you come across a real shit, who cheats and does every thing he can to upset you. I've met a few and I can recognise them. This guy Luke is one. My other coach at home, Charlie, says they'll get angry and end up psyching themselves out of it. I get mad waiting for that to happen. And we're here for a whole bloody week.'

Uncle Joe listened patiently.

'Wait and see,' he said, 'you know Hans well enough to have a word with him if you want to.'

'No thanks, I'll solve this on my own,' I said, a bit rudely.

What was already on my mind was something different. I knew I wanted to be friends with Caroline. I was certain somehow that Luke was going to get in the way.

'By the way,' said Joe, 'you ought to call him Luc, the French way, not Luke.'

It was on the tip of my tongue to say that I'd call him whatever I liked, but I managed not to.

3 … SUNDAY EVENING

They didn't have supper at the hotel till eight o'clock. I remembered that I'd got some chocolate in my room. I needed a shower but, first, I needed a toilet; it was only a few doors along the corridor. I'd taken shoes and socks off and started to undress.

'It doesn't matter,' I thought to myself, 'I can go like this.'

I padded along the corridor in shorts and bare feet, carrying my bar of Cadbury's Bournville. I've always liked dark chocolate better than milk, like Uncle Joe with his HobNobs.

I locked the door and stood breaking the end two chunks off the bar. Splash, they fell straight into the bowl. I said some bad words. What a waste! Someone tried the handle of the door; I wondered if they'd heard me swearing.

I broke off two more bits carefully and chewed them as I stood there. The double piece in the pan looked really funny, as though somebody had a serious tummy problem. I flushed the loo. A rush of water foamed through the bowl. Afterwards, the chocolate was still there, a neat double dark brown rectangle.

'Damn.'

The tank was refilling desperately slowly. I tore off lots of paper from the roll, screwed it up and chucked it in, half filling the pan. I was worried that I'd overdone it and might make the loo overflow.

I waited patiently, hearing the water run in to the tank. The door handle was tried again. I heard a softly spoken 'merde'. I didn't know many French swear words but everyone seems to use that one.

I flushed again. All the paper went, but not the chocolate!

I couldn't hear anyone in the passage so I went out quickly and headed back to my room, carrying the rest of the chocolate. I got to the door.

'I don't believe it!' I'd left the key inside the room and locked myself out.

At that moment Caroline appeared. She walked past me smiling.

'Bonsoir.'

'Yes. Bon soir,' I replied. I stood fiddling in my pocket, pretending to look for a key which wasn't there. I might have guessed she would be the one who had been trying the door. And she would see the dark brown squares and wonder.

I shot downstairs and bumped straight into Hans. I explained what had happened, about the key, not the chocolate. He found a spare in the reception desk and told me to put it back later. As I got to the top of the stairs, still dressed only in shorts, Caroline was coming out of the loo, laughing out loud. I must have gone the reddest red that I've ever gone in my whole life. She must know it was me. She'd think I was deformed, abnormal.

I ran past her, mumbling something incoherent, unlocked my door and shot into the room. I slammed the door and collapsed on the bed.

There was nothing I could do. I could hardly ask Uncle Joe to explain to Caroline in French, probably over supper. I didn't even want to have to tell him about it. But I did want to get to know Caroline better. I'd have to try to speak some French, or persuade her to practise her English.

I dragged off the rest of my clothes and wandered into the shower. The flow of water was not enough for me to be able to drown myself, which I probably ought to have considered. After I'd done enough soaping and shampooing to smell reasonable, I grabbed the only towel. It didn't even reach round my waist. I thought Uncle Joe might be a bit out of his depth here; he was used to much smarter places.

I switched on the television and lay on the bed. All the programmes were in Italian except one which was probably German.

I must have dropped off because the next thing I knew there was a knock at the door.

'Le dîner est servi. Tu es prêt?' It was Joe.

'Quoi? Hang on.'

I unlocked the door, trying to hold on to the towel, which was still all I had on.

'In case you didn't understand, I asked if you were ready. Apparently not!'

'I'll only be two seconds,' I replied. As I dressed quickly, I told him about the key problem and meeting Caroline twice. Even though I didn't mention the chocolate, I went red again as I told him.

'It was really embarrassing to be out in the passage half-naked.'

'So what? That doesn't sound too disastrous to me,' was his attitude. 'Elle va te voir bientôt en caleçon de bain, in swimming trunks.' But he did do a lot of laughing.

'When you've got to know the young lady a bit better, you'll be able to have a good giggle together.'

Supper was served on the terrace. The others were all already there, Hans and Ilse together at a large table. Caroline was next to Hans and then a very smart lady, who I guessed must be Caroline's mother. They had similar looks, but her Mum used lots of artificial aids, make-up, eye shadow, all those things. I wouldn't be surprised if her hair was a wig.

Luc and Claudia were with them too.

'I didn't know if you would want to join us. If you will, we'll arrange a bigger table for tomorrow,' said Hans.

'Yes, thank you,' said Joe. 'Paul will get bored with my company.'

We sat down at a small table, next to theirs.

They went on talking, mainly in French.

'Uncle, you're going to have to listen in, and tell me if there's anything I ought to know.'

'But that's rude,' he replied.

'No, please. I have to know if Caroline's talking about ... you know what.'

'Locking yourself out is not such a big deal,' he laughed. Of course I hadn't told him about the chocolate. 'And stop calling me Uncle.'

The first course was meant to be soup but it was so thin, you'd hardly have guessed.

'Buon appetito,' said Hans from the next table. 'That's Italian for bon appetit in case you hadn't guessed.'

'Even I could have worked that out,' I said.

We had two little pieces of pork, which would have been ideal to repair your shoes. With that, there was plain spaghetti, with no sauce. Joe asked for tomato ketchup.

'C'est bon,' he said, 'il faut que je perdes du poids ... I need to lose some weight.'

'What are they talking about?' I asked again quietly.

He looked uncomfortable.

'I can't listen in and repeat it all. Be patient; we'll go for a walk after supper, pour aider notre digestion, to aid our digestion.'

I laughed. 'I just hope you've got a good enough memory.'

We had another bottle of white wine and I was allowed to help drink it. That was the sort of thing where Uncle Joe was different from Mum and Dad. With them alcohol was pretty much out of the question. Then there was dessert, just ice cream, plain vanilla, but very white, not creamy like it is at home and no way up to the standard of our Coupe Denmark.

The others had been talking solidly, in French and German. I got the impression that Ilse and Claudia didn't speak French. Almost every time I turned to look at them, I caught Claudia's eye.

To make matters worse, Luc seemed to be getting all Caroline's attention.

Hans suggested we join them for coffee. They made some space and we pulled our chairs across.

'Vous avez bien mangé,' asked Hans.

Joe looked at me.

'Er ... yes, it was fine.'

'No,' said Joe, 'Paul is being polite. Nous n'avons pas bien mangé. But we'll survive. It's good for my figure, and he's spoilt at home, so it'll do him good.

'Now, tell us about tomorrow.'

Hans apologised that food was not the hotel's strong point, then he explained the programme. I waited impatiently. I wanted to get Joe away to find out what they had been talking about over supper.

'Well, young man, we were going to have a walk to aid the digestion of that meal,' he joked finally.

We wandered off along the terrace.

'I thought we'd never get away. Tell me,' I pleaded.

'Quoi?'

'Don't be mean; you know what I mean.'

'OK, mais en français.'

'Uncle Joe, that's not fair.'

'Uncle?'

'OK, d'accord ... Joe!'

'Alors, ils ont parlé ... translate ... '

'They have talked ... '

'... au sujet des vacances, après cette semaine de tennis.'

'... on the subject of holidays, after the tennis week. Oh, come on, this just adds to the suspense.'

'I didn't hear your name mentioned once. Luc was going on about his family having a house in the South of France; he is a bit of a pain. Claudia's off to America with her family. And ... the one you want to know about ... Caroline is going to stay with her

Grandpa. And here is the one mega-surprise. Tu le connais déjà! You know him!'

'Uncle, no, I mean Joe, you're teasing me again.''

'Pas du tout et pourquoi? On such an important subject? Guess!'

'I haven't the faintest.'

'I'll give you a clue, il vit près du même lac que moi, he lives on Lake Geneva.'

'No, the Viscount of whatsit whatsit.'

'Got it in one. Le Vicomte Jean-Marie de Launay de St.Etienne. Il est le grand-père de Caroline. She's obviously quite proud of him, and the fact that he's a bit eccentric. He's her mother's father.

'Of course you realised the glamorous lady with Caroline is her Mum. I think Mum is not so proud of her père as Caroline is of her grandpère, if you see what I mean.

'The problem seems to be that the old man is not only a banker but an important scientist, he's involved amongst other things with CERN, the place in Geneva where they've made such important discoveries.'

'Yes,' I said, 'I've read about the Higgs boson and things, it's amazing.'

'But he does a lot of really secret work and so, to avoid telling people what he does, he just tells very tall stories.'

'What, lies you mean?'

'Yes but I gather it's always clear that he's joking.'

I wondered whether he really had done work on roller skates or whether that was just a joke.

'Joe, I'm going to stay with you for a few days, aren't I, after this?'

'Yes,' he replied; 'I'd already thought of that too, but don't jump to conclusions. You may change your mind over the next few days, tu peux décider que c'est Claudia que tu préfères.'

'I bet you a hundred francs I don't and I can't fly to America to be with her!'

'French francs or Swiss ones?'

'Swiss ... they're worth more, aren't they? And anyway there aren't any French francs any more; they have euros.'

'Right! I just hope you've got the money to pay up.'

Hans and Ilse were deep in conversation when we got back. Caroline was sitting slightly apart from them; the others had gone, presumably to bed. She smiled at me.

'Viens ici,' and she waved a hand.

'Quoi?' I said nervously.

Uncle Joe walked tactfully on: 'I'm for bed. Goodnight everyone. See you at breakfast.'

I sat down on the empty chair next to Caroline.

'Je ne veux pas jouer toujours avec Luc. Je le trouve parfois ennuyant. Il faut que tu parles avec Hans.'

'Wow, that's too much,' I said. 'Encore, s'il vous plaît.'

'S'il te plaît,' she corrected me.

'Quoi?'

'Il faut que tu dises tu ... you say tu to me, not vous. Alors, s'il te plaît, not s'il vous plaît.'

This was what Joe had said. If I had to say tu to her, not vous, we were off to a good start.

'And the rest ... ?' I asked.

'Je ne veux pas ...'

'I do not wish.'

'Je ne veux pas ... jouer ... toujours ... avec Luc.'

'To play, always ... with Luc! You don't want to play with him all the time!'

'Exactement, mon ami. Tu comprends le français!'

'Yea, great, I understand a few words, provided you speak at a snail's pace.'

'Quoi?' she said with a grin.

31

'Oh, gee, this is silly ... I understand ...'

'Je comprends, non c'est toi, tu comprends ...'

'Provided, no, if ...'

'Si ...'

'You speak ...'

'Tu parles, non, je parle ...' she giggled.

'Like a snail ... wait, I know that word, comme un escargot!'

'Quoi? Je ne comprends pas, pas du tout!'

We both started laughing. She tried English.

'You say I am un escargot, a snail?'

She managed to pronounce snail as though it rhymed with smile.

'No, no, non, non. Demain, ... I'll explain demain.' I thought I could get Joe to help.

'OK et d'accord.'

We both started to move at the same moment. We walked up the stairs together. She turned to say good night and offered a hand.

'Bonne nuit et dors bien.'

'Oui ... non ... quoi?'

I took the offered hand and pretended to kiss it goodnight. She blushed and we both laughed.

I unlocked my door, went into the room, and leapt about three feet in the air.

'Wow ... !'

4 … MONDAY

The following morning I still felt pretty good. I had an extra long shower, soaped myself like mad, and then used a bottle of Dad's after-shave which I'd borrowed. I don't shave yet, but it was the only spare anything that might smell good.

We still had our separate table for breakfast.

'A quelle heure vas-tu jouer?' asked Joe.

'Neuf heures,' I replied. 'Till twelve; it'll be a long morning in this heat.'

I told him that Caroline had asked me to make sure she didn't have to play with Luc all the time.

'Now I realise why you smell different,' he laughed. 'Quel arôme!'

'I thought you might speak to Hans for me.' I tried one of my winning smiles.

'Cor, I have to do your dirty work for you, to help your love affair.'

I blushed again but I decided he'd probably try to help.

We all arrived for tennis on time. Caroline hadn't appeared for breakfast; she'd probably had some in her bedroom. I'd soon be really sweaty and the after-shave would be wasted.

She smiled at me and I managed a bonjour.

'Bonjour, Monsieur Nike!' said Hans.

I wasn't wearing Nike gear today, except a cap, but it didn't make any difference to the nick-name he had chosen.

'Non,' said Luc. 'Il n'est pas Monsieur Nike; il est Monsieur Merde Carrée!'

Hans laughed. 'Pourquoi?'

'What's he on about?' I had understood one word. I knew that merde was the one rude word in French that everyone seemed to use.

'What was the other word?' I asked Hans.

'Carré means square,' he replied. 'I don't understand either.'

Now I did understand. Merde carrée, something you'd see in a toilet bowl, but square. Caroline was laughing too; she stopped when she saw the expression on my face. I must have looked as though I was going to explode.

'Forget it,' I said fiercely to Hans; he got the message.

'OK, on joue au tennis. Let's play tennis.'

'How could she?' I said to myself. To tell Luc of all people. Two-faced, that's what she was. But Hans didn't seem to understand, so she couldn't have told all of them. Did that mean she'd been alone with Luc. When? Where?

'Hallo, Paul. Tu es là? Are you with us?'

'Sorry, what?'

'Try and stay on the same planet with us, please,' said Hans.

The first part of the morning was a series of exercises, like yesterday, but more of it. Hans was a sadist, making us do push-ups if we made bad mistakes. He was much tougher on me and Luc than the girls. He explained that long ago as a junior he had had coaching from Niki Pilic, the first captain to win the Davis Cup five times, with three different countries, Germany, Croatia and Serbia.

'Mister Pilic made me do push-ups; that's what great coaching is all about!' he laughed.

I wanted to look for Luc's weaknesses, so that I could thrash him later. After a long time, Hans told us to play some singles. Luc was soon cheating again. I put up with it for a little while.

'Deux partout,' he said.

That must mean two games all.

'D'accord,' I agreed.

He smirked as he repeated d'accord; he was mocking my accent.

He served an ace down the centre line.

'Fault, or faute if you prefer.'

'Non,' he screamed at once; 'c'était bon.'

He crossed over to serve to the backhand court. I stood where I was, waiting for a second serve. Hans was on the next court with the girls; he was keeping an eye on us.

'C'était bon, on continue,' said Luc.

'Non, c'est à moi, it's my call,' I replied loudly. Hans came over.

Luc spoke to him in French, very fast so I wouldn't know what he was saying. Hans must have told him that it was my call. He finally put his second serve into the net, obviously on purpose.

'Satisfait?'

'Oui, merci,' I replied.

'Alors, pas de discussion, on joue. There's no need for argument,' said Hans.

Luc was now rattled. He lost that game. Then he tried to call one of my ground shots long, but Hans overruled him.

'Mais, ça, ce n'est pas juste. Tu prends son côté.'

'No, I'm not on his side. The ball was good.'

'Merde!' Then he remembered.

'Ha, merde carrée!'

That made me angry. Fortunately Hans called a halt before we came to blows.

'Café,' he said. 'Et, si vous voulez, cinq minutes dans la piscine.'

Luc went and dived straight into the pool.

'He should take a shower before,' said Hans. 'He takes all his sweat into our pool, the bad boy.'

I grinned. 'You can say that again.'

'Quoi?' asked Caroline.

'Nothing, rien.'

The coffee break was not a happy occasion. I wanted to talk to Caroline but not in front of the others. Luc had been told off by Hans for not having a shower. Dominique joined us and said what a coincidence it was that I'd met her father, the Vicomte, even sat next to him on the flight.

'But that is not regular,' said Luc. 'You have said yesterday that you voyaged as a child, n'est-ce pas? It is not permitted to sit with an adult.'

Joe understood what he was talking about and explained.

'Yes, unaccompanied minors, there are rules like that. But I guess the airline knows the Vicomte well enough.'

'Il faut porter plainte,' said Luc.

'No,' said Joe firmly enough to end the coffee break, 'we shall not complain.'

After our coffee break, when we played doubles, Hans changed the partners. Joe must have had that promised word with him. But Claudia said she didn't feel well so Hans took her place. This meant we didn't have a serious game but Caroline and I managed to play as a real pair. I've played with girl partners before and often they keep a second service ball tucked in their underwear. I think it looks odd but you even see it sometimes at Wimbledon. My partner's shorts had pockets … alors pas de problème!

Some of my friends claim to have been going out with girls for ages. The stories they tell are fairly outrageous. I don't believe half of them. I've always been a bit shy and I told you about my blushing problem. I have to say that Caroline was really the first girl I'd been properly interested in.

I was getting fed up waiting for a chance to talk to her alone. Lunch seemed to drag on.

'Shall we go for a walk,' I suggested as soon as she'd finished a nectarine, which was today's dessert.

'Pas de café?'

'No, thanks, I don't want any. But you can ...'

'Non, OK, je viens.'

We got up. As we walked away, she looked at me without smiling.

'Alors, tu veux dire quelque chose?'

'Yes.' Now that we were alone, I didn't know where to begin.

'En français?'

'No, I'll speak in English, you can speak French. That way we both learn.'

'D'accord.'

'You've been talking to Luke.'

'Luc,' she corrected me.

'Oui, et pourquoi pas? Tu parles aussi avec lui.'

'Yes, OK, I know, I talk to him as well, but only because I have to.'

'Et il faut que je l'ignore? Pourquoi?'

'Quoi?'

'Ignorer ... c'est le même mot en anglais, n'est-ce pas?'

'Ignore, yes. And no, you don't have to ignore him. But don't talk about me.'

'Quoi? Quoi?'

'You did, you know you did. You told him about the toilet.'

She looked puzzled.

I tried in French: 'la toilette.' She laughed.

'C'était amusant, ton chocolat.'

'Why tell him?'

'Pourquoi pas?'

'It should be private. I was very embarrassed.'

'Mais non, comme tu es enfantin.'

'Quoi?' I was sure this was mean, but I wasn't sure what she'd said.

'Enfantin, tu es enfantin. I do not know in English. Comme un enfant, you are like a child.'

'Merde,' I swore.

She turned on her heel and walked away.

'Brilliant, Paul, just brilliant,' I said to myself. I'd really handled that well. I hadn't even told her ... the only thing which really made me mad was the stupid name that Luc had dreamed up, Monsieur Merde Carrée.

I couldn't go back to the table; I didn't know where she would have gone. I went up to my room and lay on the bed. After about five minutes I had a bright idea.

I went along and knocked on Joe's door.

'Entrez.'

He was sitting at the table, tapping away on his lap-top. He's not totally retired. He writes books about finance and money management. I think they're boring. He agrees but says they pay him well.

He had Pink Floyd playing in the background, on a baby CD system. He says he hates headphones and takes it everywhere. He's weird; you never know whether it'll be Mozart or Queen. He says they're both classical.

'Hi, it's me. I'm bored and thought I could go for a ride on one of the bikes. If you don't mind.'

'You were with your new friend.'

'Yes, I was.'

There was a pause. He waited for me to say something else. I didn't oblige.

'Right.' Another pause.

'George's keys are over there. Take the Saracen, the black one. I wouldn't trust you with my Specialised.' He grinned.

'Thanks a lot.'

'And take some of that cash. Take two or three twenties.'

He meant euros of course.

'Wow, thanks.'

'It's not a gift. It's just in case you have any problems. Take your phone too, you have my number in it?'

'Yes, OK, but I'm not sure I've got the right roaming deal.'

'Any way, get back by half three, and we'll have a drink on the terrace. I'll need a break and you may be just a tad more talkative.'

'Right. And thanks Joe, you're my favourite uncle.'

He knows, of course, that I only have one uncle.

Inside the Discovery it was like a sauna. The bikes were hot to the touch. I pulled the Saracen out and locked up again.

From the terrace of the hotel, you could see the town below, down by the lake. Since the lake was called Garda, it wasn't too surprising that the town was called Garda too. There seemed to be several roads and paths going down so I just followed my nose.

There were lots of cafes with tables by the lake. I bought an ice cream cone, dark chocolate of course, and sat on a seat.

Chocolate, that was what had caused my problems. I'd been an idiot. Why had I got cross with Caroline? Even Luc might not perhaps be quite as objectionable as I'd thought. I know plenty of other boys who cheat at tennis, given half the chance. My coaching had taught me how to deal with it.

This was still only the first day. Play it cool! I could cope with Monsieur Luc and get to know Caroline as well.

I watched the world go by. It seemed as though roller blades had just arrived in Garda. Nearly all the boys and lots of the girls had them. I thought about the new invention I'd seen on the flight out. If it worked, he'd probably make a fortune ... again!

It had been all downhill from the hotel. It had to be solid climb all the way back. I found a different path back, off-road, which was good, but I was sweating like mad when I arrived. As I rode along the last level stretch towards the hotel, I met Luc walking the other way. He tried to hide the cigarette he was smoking but he knew I'd seen it.

'Tu veux une cigarette?'

'No. Non, merci. Je ne fume pas. Je ne fume jamais.'

'OK, comme tu veux.'

I was quite pleased with my French. He was looking at the bike.

'Bon vélo, ça. Saracen, c'est une bonne marque.'

'Oui,' I said lamely.

'Alors. A bientôt.' He wandered on.

I must remember "à bientôt"; it was like "see you". It made a change from "au revoir".

Joe was sitting on the terrace with a drink. I grinned at him and flicked sweat off my face. I told him where I'd been and about the roller-bladers.

But my mind was still on sorting things out with Caroline.

'Tell me please, Joe, how to apologise in French.'

'There are lots of ways. Excusez-moi, je suis désolé, that's a good one ... they use that a lot. It's like saying I am desolated. But you'll have to tell me why.'

I brought him up to date, about Luc's stupid nick-name and my getting cross with Caroline.

'I have to apologise to her. She said I was being childish and, well, I suppose I was.'

Suddenly I realised that he didn't know about the chocolate. I blushed all over again as I explained.

'I thought you'd get around to telling me. I'd already heard from Hans. Luc told him.'

'Shit,' I said; 'does everyone know?'

'OK, enough. It's no big deal, let's work something out.'

He was doing a crossword, and so he tore off a piece of the paper.

'Je suis desolé, Caroline ... then what?'

'To have been so stupid?'

' ... d'avoir parlé d'une manière si stupide! Can you work that out?'

'Yes, I think so. I am desolated that I have spoken in a manner so stupid, in such a stupid way. But I'll never remember all that. You'll have to write it all down.'

He laughed and did as I'd asked.

'Go and get ready or you'll be late again. And ... have you phoned home yet?'

'Oh damn, no. I'll do it tonight before supper. They'll be going mad.'

'I'll get blamed too. You know your Mum doesn't think you're safe with me!'

'I hope she's right.' I ran up to my room, clutching the note he'd written.

Tennis that afternoon wasn't bad; we managed to avoid any real unpleasantness. I was waiting for my chance to apologise to Caroline.

The only event of the session involved Claudia. She made a fuss about who she was going to hit with and then again about who was to be her partner in the doubles. It did seem that she was trying to fix to be with me all the time. Hans got cross and told her to do what she was told.

'It's always the same,' she screamed. 'You just pick on me because I'm black.'

'Rubbish,' replied Hans. 'I bet you always use that as an excuse when you don't get your own way.'

'We're paying to be here,' she screamed, 'you can't talk to me like that!'

'I just did,' he smiled. 'You decide what you want to do.'

It seems silly to say that I hadn't really noticed she was black, but it's true. I decided to try to be nicer to her any way. But life was going to be tough if I had to be nice to everybody.

5 … MONDAY EVENING

That night, for supper, we were all at the same table. I ended up with Caroline on one side and Claudia on the other. I didn't get a chance to talk to Caroline alone beforehand. Uncle Joe seemed to be getting on very well with Caroline's Mum.

Luckily most of the conversation was in English.

'Paul went down to Garda this afternoon on his bike,' Joe told everybody.

'It was good but quite a struggle coming back up,' I said.

'Mais ça, c'est un bon vélo. Je l'ai vu. Plusieurs vitesses,' said Luc.

'Yes, it's quite fast,' I agreed.

'Not speed, Paul, that means many gears. N'est-ce pas, Luc, comme vingt-et-une vitesses?'

'Oui, exactement.'

'Oh, right, yes, twenty-one.'

By now I'd learned that Caroline's Mum was called Dominique. 'Mais ça c'est pas possible,' she laughed. 'Ma petite voiture n'a que cinq vitesses!'

'Mais oui,' said Luc, 'le moteur d'un vélo est humain, n'est ce pas? On a besoin de plus de vitesses. Trois fois sept c'est normal.'

Hey, I thought to myself, I'm beginning to understand more of their conversation, in French. A bike needs more gears because it's engine is a person.

Then Dominique had a bright idea : 'Tu peut l'accompagner,' she said to Caroline, 'la prochaine fois'.

I understood this too, that I could have company next time, but Caroline looked a bit doubtful. I wondered why; she was probably still cross with me. Maybe she just didn't want Mum interfering; I could understand that.

'Ça serait possible,' said Joe, 'nous avons deux vélos.'

'Those bikes can be dangerous,' said Claudia, 'I knew somebody who had a really bad accident. And you,' she said turning to me, 'I saw you, not even wearing one of those safety hats.'

Later Joe asked Caroline what she was doing after the tennis week. She didn't understand his English. Her Mum said they were going to stay with the Vicomte on Lake Geneva.

The food was no better this evening. Somehow, being with a crowd of people, it didn't seem to matter so much. I'm sure Joe was hating it, but he didn't let it show. My glass kept getting refills from all directions. Tonight it was red wine, which I haven't had very often before.

Then I did something really stupid. I often tip back on chairs at home and Dad gives me a hard time.

'You'll break that chair one day,' is his normal line.

But at home I'm not normally holding a glass of wine.

The inevitable happened. The chair didn't go right over; I stopped it in time. But the wine flew out of the glass, straight up in the air, and down into my lap. There was a chorus of shouts and laughter in French and English. I was still wearing white tennis shorts; they were fast going bright pink.

'Il faut aller se changer, c'est du vin rouge qui va tacher les shorts,' said Joe.

'No,' said Hans, 'go down by the pool and stick your shorts under the shower. They'll dry on you. You won't get pneumonia here!'

There were underwater lights in the pool but it was quite dark by the shower. I whipped my shorts off and let them really soak in the cold water. Just as I decided they were clean enough, there was a flash, like lightning. I knew at once what it was, but I couldn't see a thing.

I put the wet shorts back on. I wondered if they went see-through when they were wet. At the table, they were all roaring with laughter. I tried to join in; maybe the shorts really were see-through!

'Who was that?' I shouted. 'I bet it was Joe ... or Hans.'

There was no reply, only more laughter. But Hans had left his camera on the table in front of him. He'd probably already passed it round the table for everybody to look at.

'I shall sell the picture to the newspapers,' he said, 'but only after you have won the men's final at Wimbledon. Then I shall make lots of money.'

Joe helpfully changed the subject for me.

'Paul, I bet you still haven't phoned home. It's not too late because we're an hour ahead of them here. Take my phone and it's probably best to call from your room.'

I ran up the stairs. Joe had written down earlier what to dial for the UK. I tried to do it as quickly as I could. I didn't want to find that Caroline had gone to bed by the time I got back downstairs. While I was dialling and getting through I found some other shorts, dry ones.

'Dad, hi, it's me.'

'Yes, good, how's it going?'

Before I had time to tell him, he said he'd put Mum on the line ...

'Otherwise you'll have to tell it all twice. She'll tell me and the others.'

'OK, Dad, thanks, 'bye.'

'Hello, dear,' said Mum, 'we were wondering when you'd ring. Are you having a lovely time?'

I told her quickly about the journey out and the hotel.

'My room's so small I can touch both walls at the same time.'

'Well I expect that keeps the price down, dear.'

'I don't think Joe likes it much, Mum.'

'It will be good for him to stay somewhere cheaper, he's used to so much luxury in Switzerland.'

She really is a bit unfair on Uncle Joe.

'And I don't really think you ought to be calling him Joe, dear,' she went on.

'But he told me to, Mum.'

'Well, it's up to him, but it seems a bit funny to me,' she replied.

I asked about Ben, our sheep-dog, and then Richard and Sophie, my little brother and sister. I'd always ask about the dog first!

I remembered the problem at the airport.

'By the way, Mum, I wanted to say how really sorry I am, honestly, about ...'

I heard a sort of gasp at the other end of the line.

'I told Joe not to tell you.'

I was totally confused.

'What about?'

There was a long silence.

'What were you saying sorry for, dear?' she asked.

'About the fuss I made at the airport, with the silly label. What are you talking about?'

'Sorry, dear, nothing. It was a mistake.'

'Mum, you cannot do that. Something bloody has happened ... you've got to tell me.'

'Don't swear, dear.'

'Mum ...' I screamed down the 'phone. 'Tell me!'

'No dear, trust me. I'm not going to spoil your holiday.'

'OK, fine, I'll ring you again some time. Bye.'

You've already spoiled the holiday, thanks a million. I'd quickly disconnected the call but I felt a bit sorry for Mum.

What had happened? All sorts of horror stories careered through by brain. Sophie or Richard had had an accident, Ben had been run over, Dad had been made redundant. Mum was going to have another baby!

'Stop it, you idiot,' I said to myself. 'Joe will tell me.'

Halfway downstairs I realised I still hadn't changed the wet shorts. No matter. I shot out on to the terrace. Hans and Ilse were there, with Caroline. The others had gone.

'Where's Joe?' I asked Hans.

'He's taken Caroline's Mum down to Garda for a drink. We were keeping Caroline company till you came back.'

'Merde,' I said loudly.

'What's the problem?'

'No,' I said, 'it's nothing.' Life was getting too complicated. I still had to go through with my apology to Caroline. How could I concentrate and have a panic about home at the same time?

I sat down beside Caroline.

'Je vais t'acheter une boisson,' said Hans, 'et puis nous allons nous coucher. Qu'est -ce que tu veux? Coca normal ou peut-être quelque chose de plus fort? Something strong, I think?'

'No, thanks, I've had stacks of red wine. Just a Coke, that'd be brilliant. Merci. Or even s'il vous plaît.'

I turned to look at Caroline. She was looking amused and puzzled. She waited patiently for me to say or do something. I remembered a bit of my script.

'Je suis desolé ...' I grinned. She smiled at me.

'Oui, mais pourquoi?'

I put my hand in my still wet pocket. I pulled out the most unpleasant looking piece of paper imaginable.

'Merde, I can't read it.'

Caroline was now laughing out loud. We smoothed the paper out on the table.

'Je suis desolé,' ... I could not read it ... 'je suis très desolé ... absolutely desolé ...'

' ... absolument ... absolument désolé ...' she giggled.

There was a candle on the table; I held the soggy scrap up to the light.

'Mais, oui,' I cried. I stood up, then knelt on the ground at her side.

'Je suis desolé, Caroline, ... que j'ai parlé d'une manière si stupide!'

She roared with laughter.

'Excellent, merci, mais ... '

She was looking over my shoulder. I turned, still on my knees. The waiter was standing behind me with my Coke. He was grinning too.

'You like your drink down there?'

We all laughed.

'Non, merci, sur la table, s'il vous plaît.'

Caroline grabbed both my hands and pulled me to my feet.

'Now, please, sit.' Her eyes were sparkling, mean girl, she was loving this.

'Alors, il faut expliquer. Tu es désolé. Pourquoi?'

'You know. Because ...' No, blast it, tell her in French.

'En français ... je suis desolé ... what's because? ... parce que ... j'étais un enfant, comme un enfant, enfantin, comme tu as dit.'

'Bravo!' She leaned forward and kissed me lightly on the cheek. I thought this was amazing but then I remembered that the French do kiss each other all the time.

'Mais, maintenant, tu as téléphoné, tu as parlé à ta maman. Il y a un problème?'

This was stunning, a whole sentence in French which I understood. She knew that I'd telephoned home. She knew there was a problem.

'Il y a un grand problème, but I have no idea what it is, j'ai aucune idée qu'est-ce que c'est.'

I told her slowly in English what had happened, that Mum had misunderstood me, and let the cat out of the bag. It took quite a while to make her understand about cats and bags! We'd already had the "snail" problem, when I'd suggested she should speak comme un escargot!

'So now it is necessary to wait for Joe, yes?'

'Oui,' I agreed, 'il faut attendre.'

'S'attendre,' she corrected me.

I sipped my Coke. It was really cold with lots of ice, and a slice of lemon.

'You want a drink?'

'Yes, please.' She picked up my glass and had a sip.

'No, no, I meant please can I buy you a drink.'

Now she looked really embarrassed.

'Excuse-moi! Je suis désolé. J'ai pensé ...'

Silly girl, she thought I didn't like her drinking from my glass! I put my hand on hers.

'It doesn't matter. I would love to share this one, if you don't mind.'

I went red too! This was the moment that Joe and Caroline's Mum chose to come back. We must have looked pretty silly, both of us with bright red faces.

Caroline broke the silence: 'Alors, je vais me coucher. Bonne nuit.' She blew me a kiss and smiled at the others. Her mother said good night too and followed her.

Joe sat down beside me.

'So, it looks like your evening has gone well!'

'Yes, Joe, thanks.' I wasn't sure how to tackle him. I'd already worked out that he'd probably refuse to tell me whatever it was.

'How was yours?'

'We had a drink in one of those cafes down by the lake. It's really nice down there in the evening, with lots of people wandering up and down. Caroline's mother is very pleasant. She has quite a wild social life in Paris.'

'So you'll be going to see her?' We knew Caroline's father had left them years ago.

'Pourquoi tu peux penser ça? I was only chatting the lady up for your benefit, to get us both out of your way!'

'Gee thanks Joe.'

'Paul, what is it? You're in a state. What's happened? You looked as though you were getting on pretty well.'

I hadn't realised my face gave the game away so much.

'It's nothing to do with Caroline. I was upset by what Mum said, you know, the problem, at home.'

'What problem?' he asked, looking suddenly very serious.

'You know what I mean. It's awful, isn't it?'

It wasn't going to work, I knew.

'I don't know, because you don't know, young man. Please explain what happened, exactly, when you rang them.'

I told him how Mum had obviously put her foot in it, and then refused to tell me any more.

'She said she didn't want to spoil my holiday. I mean that's just stupid."

'So you thought you'd trick it out of me?'

'No, Joe, not a trick, I just have to know.'

'Of course it was a trick, and that doesn't make me feel very good.'

'OK. I'm sorry. Bloody hell, I'm spending this whole trip apologising for things. Please tell me what's going on.'

'Paul, I can't. Whatever it is, if Judith won't tell you, I can't.'

Judith is my Mum's name, as if you hadn't guessed.

'Merde, merde, merde, mille fois merde. This is unbelievable. Give me a clue. Is anybody dead?'

'Nobody's dead, no body nor the dog, as far as I know. I will not answer any more questions. I promise I will telephone them and sort something out.'

'What?'

'Don't be silly, I don't know what till I've done it.'

'But Mum'll be awkward, like she always is. She doesn't even like you,' I blurted out.

'That doesn't help. What do you mean?'

'You must know. She thinks Dad's jealous of you, she reckons he'd rather have your life.'

'And you, what do you think?'

I knew I'd been stupid.

'I don't think anything.'

Joe smiled pleasantly. I put an arm round his enormous shoulders.

'You're my favourite uncle. But you do have to do your sorting out for me. Like now.'

'Non, je suis vraiment désolé mais c'est trop tard. You're going to have a miserable night, but I promise I'll call them first thing in the morning.'

We walked upstairs together. He was right, I was going to have a hard time getting to sleep.

6 ... TUESDAY

I didn't get to sleep until I'd been through a whole range of lunatic ideas as to what might have happened at home. I woke up early but I knew there was no point in bullying Joe. It was too early; he couldn't phone them yet because of the time difference. I tried reading but I couldn't concentrate.

Then I had a bright idea. I pulled on a pair of swimming shorts, grabbed a towel, didn't forget the key, and went downstairs. There was no-one about. I slid into the pool at the shallow end and shivered. It gets so hot in Italy during the day, they don't bother to heat their pools. I did six lengths of steady crawl.

I saw that Luc was watching me from his bedroom window. Just as I was about to wave, he disappeared. I did a few more lengths expecting he might come down.

Back in my room I had a long shower. I was a bit gentler with the after-shave, put on the day's tennis kit, and went along to Joe's room. I tapped on the door.

'I'd been sitting here a while,' he said, 'expecting you to knock at any moment but then I looked outside and saw where you were.'

I opened my mouth to speak, but ...

'Yes, I've rung them. I've had a long chat with your Mum. She knew you'd bully me. It was a friendly chat! She realises this is all her fault.'

'And ... now you can tell me.'

'Yes, she told me to use my own judgment.' He laughed.

'Go on, s'il te plaît,' I pleaded.

'I knew you weren't telling the truth last night. You kept saying your Mum was talking about a problem. It's all very sad, but it ain't no problem. I'm afraid I lied to try and stop you worrying. Your Gran's died, my Mum.'

'Oh God, Joe ... I really am sorry.' This was the first death in my family since I'd been around. I felt all full up inside, but I didn't want to cry in front of Joe.

'Paul, she was very old. She'd said lots of times she wanted to go. She was looking forward to seeing Dad again.'

He meant Grandpa Harry, who'd died quite a long time ago; I think it was cancer. Dad and Joe hardly remembered him.

'Joe, she wasn't really old enough. Do you think she will see him again?'

'Je n'ai aucune idée, Paul, mais elle était certaine ... and that's what counts.'

He had a great big smile on his face, but tears were rolling down his cheeks.

'Joe, ouf, je suis tellement désolé ...' I put an arm round the big shoulders again, just like last night. Now I was crying as well.

'Don't worry, old boy, I shall be fine in a minute, after we've had the day's first dose of caffeine. What on earth will the others think if they see us both sobbing our hearts out?'

'But Joe, why did all this have to be kept secret from me? J'ai presque quatorze ans, je ne suis pas un bébé!'

'Your Mum and Dad talked about it and didn't want to tell you yet. They had to fix the funeral and things. They told me the other night when I rang to say that we'd got here safely.'

If the funeral was going to be this week, Joe would have to fly back and could hardly leave me behind.

'Je veux venir,' I said.

'I bet Gran would prefer you to be playing tennis.'

'Maybe, but Joe I want to, s'il te plaît.'

'And leave Caroline?' he asked with a smile.

'Yes, definitely, and that was a rotten question.'

'OK,' he grinned.

'Any way, the funeral's on Friday. Today's Tuesday. I shall have to fly out of Geneva on Thursday afternoon. Your Dad insists he's got everything under control. I'll have to leave here very early on Thursday morning.'

'Nous allons, ensemble, pas seulement toi,' I insisted.

'Well, that's up to you, I suppose,' he replied. 'But one of the reasons I took Dominique out last night was to ask her.'

'Now you're going to tell me I can stay with Caroline, as long as I want,' I moaned.

'Yes, that's broadly it. They leave here on Saturday to go and stay with the Vicomte. You'd be welcome because he's met you already. You'd probably get Napoleon's bedroom, or something!'

'Joe, don't make it worse. I'm coming with you. Je viens avec.'

I just knew that I wanted to be there. He didn't try to argue.

'OK, but you've got to make the best of the next two days. I'll probably fly back out to Geneva on Saturday. I can't think they'll agree to you coming over again just for a couple more days. It's going to cost an arm and a leg to change your ticket.'

'I'd love to stay here but I'd rather come with you, even if it costs.'

He had already shaved and dressed before I'd knocked on his door. He must have 'phoned Mum very early.

'If we go down now, we can probably persuade them to give us some breakfast.'

The hotel was still pretty dead. After a while Joe got his coffee, and sighed with relief. I ordered a Coke.

'I'll ask Hans to make sure you get as much tennis as possible. And I'll ask Dominique to explain to Caroline, so you don't have to waste hours telling her in French!'

'Thanks, Joe.'

Luc came and sat at our table.

'Je peux t'accompagner cet après-midi, peut-être?' he asked. 'Vous avez deux vélos, n'est-ce pas?'

This I understood. He wanted to keep me company in the afternoon, because we had two bicycles. Of course I had other ideas.

'Oui,' I replied, determined to try to talk to him in French. 'Mais, j'ai demandé a Caroline, no, j'ai invité Caroline, ... déjà.'

'J'ai entendu sa mère, mais j'ai pensé que ça n'intéressait pas beaucoup Caroline. Elle ne semblait pas pleine d'enthousiasme.'

He'd obviously been listening when Caroline's Mum had told her she ought to keep me company. Joe came to my aid.

'Why not let Luc know later? See what Caroline wants to do.'

I must have looked relieved. He turned to Luc.

'Tu as compris?'

'Yes, thank you, I understand,' said Luc clearly in English.

'Je crois que c'est possible, on peut louer un troisième vélo, ou même un quatrième pour Claudia aussi. Il faut pas oublier nos amis!'

He knew I wouldn't understand and watched my expression as Joe translated. I guessed I wasn't going to like it.

'He suggests that if Caroline does want to go, we ought to hire bikes for him and Claudia.'

I'd understood that last bit, 'one mustn't forget one's friends.'

'Leave it to me,' said Joe, 'I'll make enquiries this morning.'

'But ...' and then I shut up.

The morning went quite well. We ended up with a mixed four and Caroline was my partner. The others were quite pleasant even though they lost. They all knew about Gran; Hans must have passed the word around.

At lunch, Joe said he'd made enquiries and there were not any bikes for hire.

'That's right,' said Hans. 'We've thought about getting some here at the hotel for guests to use.'

I wondered if Joe had warned Hans to agree. This was the first Claudia had heard about it, so the idea had to be explained to her. She spoke to Hans in German.

Hans nodded.

'Silly me, I'd forgotten.' He wasn't a very good liar.

'Claudia arrived before you; she was here when Ilse and I came back on our bikes. I'm sure Ilse won't mind if you borrow hers. Of course I don't mind.'

Joe had thought to put Hans in the picture, so that Hans wouldn't announce where you could hire bikes. But Joe didn't know that they had bikes there, already, on the premises. Damn and damn and dammit!

The conversation petered out and lunch passed off almost in silence. Lunch was cold soup, bread so dried up it must have been sunbathing all morning, and fruit which was way past its eat-by date.

I sat wondering what would happen next. Ilse always stayed by the pool. Not today! She came up to talk to Hans. It was the first time I'd seen the top half of her bikini.

'Hans has something to ask you,' said Claudia immediately.

He told Ilse about the bike idea.

'Yes, you must all go together, you'll have such a good time!' she said.

Actually she spoke in German, but I bet that it was something like that.

Joe looked at me sympathetically, but there wasn't anything he could do.

I borrowed the keys from Joe to get our two bikes out of the back of the Discovery. He followed me over to the car.

'Let me give you a hand.' Then, more quietly: 'I'm sorry, but I did my best.'

'I know. I ought to make the best of it and all that. But I've got so little time left to ...' My voice trailed away.

'We'll work something out for tomorrow. And there's no reason why you shouldn't meet her in the future. Perhaps at her Grandfather's?'

'Yes, I know, but God knows when! I'm going to have to ride Stumpy, aren't I!'

Uncle Joe had silly names for things. The Discovery was George. His bike was an old Specialised Stumpjumper Comp, so he called it Stumpy.

'Yes. Better you than any of the others. By the way, I've got a name for the Saracen, Genghis, but I don't know if it's right. Ask your history man at school if Genghis Khan was a Saracen.'

Our history teacher is actually female but Joe's old enough to assume all teachers of boys must be men.

We pushed the bikes back to the terrace. Luc and Hans arrived with the other two. Because Claudia was smaller, she got to ride the Saracen, and Caroline got lumbered with Ilse's machine. It had fat tyres but it didn't look like a mountain bike. It had one of those chain guards and a carrier on the back.

Luc grinned.

'Ça c'est pour ton bébé?', he asked Caroline, pointing at the carrier. She scowled at him without replying.

'Pardon, je m'excuse,' he smirked. He was loving the fact that he'd fouled up our afternoon.

As I was the only one who'd biked to Garda before, it made sense for me to lead the way. I set off down the rough path. Because I was still very cross, I went quite fast. After a while I stopped. Claudia arrived, stopped beside me and smiled pleasantly. Several minutes went by before the others turned up.

By now I was even more angry with myself; how I could I be so stupid as to leave Caroline behind with him?

Luc was still being smarmy. He spoke to me in English.

'We are sorry. We are slow. Caroline she has not the custom of the machine.'

'Not accustomed to it, you mean,' helped Claudia.

'I had understood, thank you,' I said. 'I'm sorry to have gone too fast.'

Caroline hadn't said a word; she just looked blank.

'You may continue with Claudia if you wish it. We will follow when we are ready,' Luc went on.

'Non, merci,' I replied; it was retaliation to speak French. 'Je sais ... non ... je connais la rue, la route.'

'No, for a path like that, we say chemin ou sentier.'

'No, we say for a path like this, not a path like that,' I said.

Caroline screamed, literally. 'Taisez-vous, tous les deux. Comme vous êtes enfantins.'

That word again, but she was right, we were being childish.

When we got to Garda, I realised that I'd given most of the euros back to Joe and I didn't have enough money for ice-creams for everybody, so Luc offered to buy them all. We rode back the easy way up the road.

That afternoon, during the tennis session, I hit the ball harder than ever before. It was a shame that practically every shot was out. When I played singles against Luc, he won 6-2, 6-1. Hans suggested that I take an early shower. Afterwards he told Joe he assumed I was upset about Gran. Hans is a nice man!

7 ... TUESDAY EVENING

I had the early shower that Hans suggested. I hung out of the window for a bit watching the others. Luc was trying to make every shot into a back-hand. He was practising top-spin on his back-hand. He wasn't very good at it.

Normally he sliced nearly all his back-hands. I began to think about tomorrow's games. We had to leave early on Thursday; I couldn't leave without beating him.

There was a knock at the door.

'Je peux entrer?' asked Joe.

'Bien sûr.'

'Mais je t'interromps ...?'

'Non, pas du tout. I was watching the others and trying to work out how to smash Luke tomorrow.'

He knew I'd deliberately pronounced the name wrongly.

'That sounds as if you're being very positive. Today's been pretty shitty hasn't it?'

I grinned. It must be good to be an uncle. Mums and Dads don't talk to you like that. I nodded in agreement.

'Joe, I haven't asked you about Gran. How come it all happened so quickly? She must have died within a few hours of me coming away.'

'I thought you might wonder about that. She'd had a fall last Thursday but they decided not to tell you. It seemed she was going to be OK, otherwise I'd have had to pull out of this trip. Then, you know how it can be with very old people. Other things suddenly started to pack up. It was as though she decided she'd had enough. Good way to go really.'

He had tears in his eyes again.

'God, I'm sorry Paul. You see, now this has happened, it makes me feel so bloody selfish. I used to come and see her quite often, but not enough.'

'Joe, she had all us lot. She wasn't lonely.'

'Yes, OK, well, I hope you're right.'

'What about tomorrow?' he asked. 'Je peux t'aider, arrêter quelque chose?'

'I'm going to try to talk to Caroline tonight. She knows we've got to go on Thursday, so I'm going to ask her to come for a ride with me, just me, tomorrow arvo.'

'Arvo ... why the Australian?'

'I didn't mean to do that. There's an Aussie guy at school and we've got infected with his slang. It drives the English teacher mad if we say "good arvo, sir!"'

'So,' I went on, 'the main thing is to make sure the others don't butt in, and to fix with Hans that I play singles with Luc tomorrow! Oh ... and I'd like a bit of time with Hans to practise serves, without the others watching.'

'Well, that sounds a reasonable plan of action. Allons-y, which means let's go for it.'

'By the way,' I asked, 'did you get on to the airline?'

'Yes. Stick some clothes on and we'll go and have a drink in Garda before supper.'

I chose a respectable shirt and smart jeans.

'You were on a cheapie ticket, on ne peut pas le changer. That means you have to pay all over again if you want to go back on a different flight.'

'Maybe Gran will have left me something in her will.' Then I quickly added: 'Sorry, that's not very nice.'

'Don't be silly, jokes don't stop because someone dies. It certainly isn't going to cost you. I'll pay if your Dad won't. Swiss were quite helpful when I explained. They are not charging as much as they might have.'

59

We drove down towards the lake in the Discovery. Suddenly Joe pulled over into a sort of a lay-by, by a factory.

'Une idée formidable!' He looked very cheerful.

'We haven't had a proper meal since we arrived. The food at the hotel's a disaster. You look respectable enough to take to a decent restaurant. We will treat ourselves to a slap-up dinner.'

'Yes, great, Joe, but ...'

'Oui, oui, oui, je sais, je vais inviter Caroline et sa mère aussi!'

'You're a genius,' I said, 'and I can get some plans made for tomorrow.'

He turned the car round and drove back up the hill. Outside the hotel there were only a few parking spaces where the car was shaded from the sun. Joe headed for one out of habit; the sun would be gone within another half hour or so.

'Allez à la terrasse et commander des boissons. Je vais téléphoner à Dominique.'

Caroline and her Mum were sharing a room. Joe and I had discovered between us that neither of them was enjoying it very much.

'What do you want? Qu'est-ce que tu veux boire?' I called out as he walked away.

'Une bière, s'il te plaît. Mais non, attends. Nous prenons George ce soir. S'il faut conduire, je prends une bière sans alcool.'

'Compris.'

He stopped and looked back.

'Vraiment? Tu as compris?'

'Oui, bien sûr, pas de problème. Une bière sans alcool pour Monsieur, et une bière avec beaucoup d'alcool pour moi!'

'Is that wise?'

As he walked away I called out 'a bientôt' but I don't think he heard. I was beginning to enjoy this funny language.

He was right, it was too early in the evening for me to be on the alcohol. When the waiter came, I ordered alcohol-free beer for both of us. When I started 'je veux commander', it reminded me of Caroline's grandfather on the aircraft. It was rude the way I'd corrected his English, but he'd been nice about it. If it hadn't been for Gran's bad timing, I might have met him again.

Joe was back before the drinks arrived.

'Alors, c'est une affaire réglée!'

'Quoi? Affair? ... what does reglée mean?'

'Don't panic. It's an expression ... it means that's all fixed. Elles sont très heureuses de nous accompagner et j'ai réservé une table dans un hôtel tout près du lac.'

The drinks arrived. The waiter poured out Joe's; I didn't wait and picked up the bottle.

He picked up his glass.

'Santé! Cheers!'

'Santé!' I replied

' ... and that's a revolting habit, Paul. It's been cool now for a while to drink out of the bottle. It must have started in the States or Australia and now everyone's at it.'

'Well it is quite cool!'

'You know "cool" is the one word that's still around from my generation. Exude coolth, that's what chaps like you do!'

'Do what?' I asked.

'Exude, give out, radiate ... coolth!   Show them who's Mr. Cool!'

'OK, but coolth?'

'One of my favourite words ... I read it in an old novel, by a chap called Howard Spring, when I was at school. I stuck it in my next essay. The English master crossed it out in red, and told me never to use it again. I've been using it ever since!'

'Coolth, brilliant, I'll use it at school ... and probably get the same result.'

'Yes, you won't win. It's not in the spell-check on my lap-top.'

'You mean it wasn't but I bet it is now,' I said.

'Dead right, I told the machine to learn it. But drink up, you'll want to go upstairs, find a mirror, check the gel, top up the after-shave. I certainly need to.'

'Yes but I bet you don't use a lot of gel?' You will guess that Joe does not have much hair left. I dodged a blow aimed for my right ear.

'Joe, I think you do fancy Dominique.'

This time I ran, towards the stairs and leapt up three at a time.

Just an hour or so earlier I'd been miserable as sin, now I was happy as could be. Then I remembered Gran again and wondered where she'd be at the moment. I'd never seen anyone dead. Did the funeral people tidy up the body? Would Gran be in a nightdress or her best clothes?

The evening went brilliantly. Caroline was quiet to begin with but Joe started telling some of his jokes, in French. She looked stunning, in black jeans, which were quite tight, and a plain white T-shirt. Like her tennis kit it didn't have any brand-name on it, but I bet it was special. We were at a super restaurant where you could eat outside on a terrace.

The others all ordered something called carpaccio to start with.

'I guess I better have the same,' I said.

'Mais tu sais qu'est-ce que c'est?' asked Caroline.

'Bien sûr,' I grinned, but I doubt she believed me. Luckily it was only later, when we were on our own, that Joe told me ... it was raw beef! I should have been sick on the spot if I'd known!

I had chicken with about three portions of potatoes and began to feel well-fed. Joe told a joke about snails, which had both Caroline and her Mum in hysterics.

'Et, je n'ai pas oublié,' laughed Caroline, 'les escargots, en anglais, you say snails!'

Like before, she said it to rhyme with 'smiles'.

Joe reminded us about tomorrow being my last day. Caroline and I agreed to go for the bike ride; Joe and Dominique would dream up reasons why we needed to go alone.

While they went on drinking espressos, we went for a walk along the front. All the Italians were doing the same. Going back in the car, Caroline and I sat in the back. She sat much closer than she had on the way down.

At the hotel our bikes were where we'd left them on the terrace. Because we'd needed the back seat for our outing, we'd had to leave them behind.

'Do you want to put these back in the car?' I asked Joe.

'No, I can't be bothered. They'll be OK. It's not going to rain and they're locked.'

All the others had gone to bed. There was no sign of the waiter. I wondered if we were all going to go upstairs together.

'Alors, bed-time,' said Dominique. 'Viens, ma petite.'

'Peut-être ... '

'Non, peut-être rien. C'est trop tard. Viens.'

She turned to us. 'Dormez bien, sleep well!'

'Yes, bonne nuit, ... '

'Paul,' said Joe, as soon as they were far enough away, 'I think you've got Dominique worried!'

'What do you mean?'

'She's not sure if her daughter's safe with you!'

He'd tried to keep a straight face, but now he roared with laughter.

We were still out on the terrace. I glanced up at the window at just the right moment. As Caroline checked the curtains, she blew me a kiss.

8 … WEDNESDAY MORNING

I was awake again ridiculously early. Today was going to be my last day with Caroline, at least for a while. But first there was tennis, I had to win. Before that, I did need help from Hans, if possible. How could I fix it?

I went down for a swim like the previous day. This time Luc was there ahead of me. I knew he'd seen me, but he didn't say anything. I swam a few lengths, very casually. He looked as though he was quite a swimmer. Finally we ended up at the same end.

'Bonjour,' I said brightly.

'Good morning,' he replied with no trace of a smile.

I couldn't resist the opportunity.

'Tu as bien mangé, yesterday, hier, le soir, ici?' I asked him.

'Yes,' he lied.

'Nous avons mangés très bien. Tu connais carpaccio?'

'Non, et ça ne m'intéresse pas.' He swam away.

'Fifteen love, at least,' I giggled happily to myself.

'No, that doesn't interest me,' he'd said.

He climbed out at the other end, grabbed his towel and disappeared. I swam a few more lengths and followed slowly.

Last night I'd intended to ring home again. As soon as I got upstairs, I dialled the number and got Mum.

'You're up bright and early, dear,' she said.

I reminded her about the time difference and then said all the obvious things about Gran.

'Yes, and I'm sorry I didn't tell you, dear, when you rang before, but I was only doing what seemed best.'

'Yes, Mum, that's fine, I understand.'

I told her about what we'd been doing ... well some of it. I mentioned the carpaccio.

'What about BSE?' she asked, 'that mad cow disease? Don't they have that in Italy?'

'Oh Mum, don't.'

'Seriously, dear, you ought to ask your uncle to check before you eat it again.'

'OK, Mum, I promise.'

'Tell me about the others, dear. I expect they're all very nice.'

'There's a nice French girl called Caroline, but I have to speak to her in French. And there's a boy Luc, who cheats, but I'll smash him before I leave.'

'Paul dear, …'

'Mum, smash him like at tennis, not like smash him in the face!'

We talked about my return, but Joe had already told them what he'd fixed.

'I'm sorry, Paul, but you won't be able to go out there again this holiday. It would be a lot of money and there won't really be time.' I wasn't surprised.

'Enjoy the rest of your holiday, dear, and lots of love.'

'Thanks, Mum. Lots of love to Richard and Sophie and everybody, and a hug for Ben, tell him he's the best, 'bye.'

Downstairs most of the others had arrived for breakfast. It was the first time Caroline and her Mum had come down. Only Claudia was missing.

'Today we have a change of plan,' said Hans. 'Because Paul has to leave tomorrow, I shall spend the first period coaching him alone.'

'Ilse va vous soigner,' he went on, looking at Caroline and Luc. 'Donc, vous pouvez prendre les deux courts là et nous allons aller jouer sur le numéro trois.'

We had not previously used the separate court, mainly because it had no shade at all.

'Brilliant, Joe, you're amazing,' I said to myself. He must have fixed it for me.

'Je ne savais pas qu'elle savait jouer au tennis,' said Luc meanly. 'Pour ça, elle porte tout un bikini, ou seulement un demi?'

'Tais-toi, Luc,' said Hans fiercely.

He'd spoken very fast. I'd got the bit about not knowing she played tennis; Joe translated later the question about whether she'd wear the whole of her bikini or only half!

Claudia arrived on the scene and wished us all a good morning.

'Paul,' said Joe, 'as Hans has just said, this is the last day of your holiday. You mustn't waste it.'

'Right, Joe. Hans has got the morning planned and Caroline ... we agreed last night ... we're going off this afternoon on the bikes, on our own.'

This sounded a bit lame, but I was trying to take the chance Joe was giving me. Luc scowled and Claudia just went on smiling.

'She's helping me with my French and I'm helping her pareillement.'

This was a good word I'd only just learned; it means 'likewise' or 'same to you'. If somebody says 'have a nice day' in French, you say pareillement. If you think somebody's said something rude in French, you just say pareillement, even if you haven't understood. Well, I think you can, any way!

On our separate court, I told Hans what I wanted to do.

'I think I can make him crack. I'm going to play everything on his back-hand, literally every shot, well almost. It's his weakest point and I'm sure I can get him rattled. He's going to want to win, badly. As long as I keep my temper, don't let him rattle me, I know I can do it.'

'Yes,' said Hans a little cautiously.

'You have to help me with the service placement. And that one that kicks the other way; can we work on that?'

I worked hard, harder probably than I ever had before. Only afterwards did I think about why it had all become so important. For Caroline? For England? For Gran?

Hans suggested we play our singles before lunch. I'm sure he wanted to get the unpleasantness over and done with. During the coffee break, he suggested the others could watch if Luc accepted a challenge from me. Luc didn't hesitate. He sprung to his feet.

'Bien sûr. Comme la Coupe Davis.'

There were a few other people in the hotel and they all seemed to realise that there was a special match going on. We finally had about twelve spectators. Hans climbed into the umpire's chair.

During the knock-up I deliberately played mainly to his forehand. He started to hit the ball really well. He looked relaxed and confident, just as I wanted. He won the toss and said he'd serve.

Then I took my big risk. I didn't put my plan into operation at all in that first game. He got three first serves in, I returned to his forehand and he hit some crisp winners. I only won one point, at the net, off the frame! I waved a hand in apology. We changed ends.

My first serve, down the centre line, was just long. The second one was in, he sliced a gentle return and I punched it away for a winner deep in his back-hand corner.

Things really started to go my way in his second service game. I managed to return every serve onto his back-hand. He was 1-2 down. Half-way through the set, he'd worked out what was happening. He tried to get his own back by playing me at my own game. But I've got a two-fisted back-hand which works. He lost the set 2-6.

He started arguing with Hans. It must have been embarrassing for the people watching. He made more mistakes each game. I even stopped playing to his back-hand all the time; he hardly noticed. It was all over; I'd won 6-2, 6-0.

I went to the net to shake hands. He walked towards me, then at the last moment veered away to his kit.

'Ce n'était pas juste,' he shouted to Hans; 'tu lui as donné ce matin un entraînement spécial, des idées nouvelles pour me battre. Pourquoi?'

He didn't wait for an answer but gathered up his spare racquets and stalked off.

'Oh dear,' said Hans. 'His tennis is not so bad but the temperament ...'

'What was his question?' I asked Joe.

'Come on, Paul ... entraînement spécial ... any ideas?'

'Special training?'

'Exactement! ... et des idées nouvelles pour me battre?'

'OK, I get it, new ideas, new ways to beat me.'

I had a shower and a swim, then took my kit up to my room. It was lucky I wasn't staying all week. I already had a pile of smelly tennis kit big enough to add to global warming.

I assumed we'd go off for our bike ride immediately after lunch. I had another shower, squirted a drop more here and there; I even sprayed a little on the used kit. There was one clean polo shirt left. Then it had to be swimming shorts; they would soon dry on me.

When Caroline appeared for lunch, I decided she'd dressed for the ride too, but a bit more stylishly than me.

She came and sat with Joe and me; he offered to get her a Coke.

'Yes, please, mais restez là. Ne bougez pas.'

'D'accord. Dis au garçon, c'est sur mon compte, numéro dix-huit.'

'Merci, Joe.'

'She is quite delightful,' said Joe as Caroline went into the bar. 'I hope you two stay friends. I was telling her this morning where you ought to go on your ride. There's a promenade thing all the way along the lake. You can stop somewhere and have a swim maybe.'

He described where he meant.

'Caroline understood; they've been there before. And you look as though you're dressed for a swim already.'

Now I understood what Caroline was wearing. From the back view, you could only see a neck strap, a tanned back and white shorts. Underneath those shorts she obviously had on a one-piece bathing suit; it was navy blue.

After lunch we sat on the terrace for coffee. Luc and Claudia had been talking quietly together; I hoped they were making their own plans for the afternoon. Caroline and Dominique were sitting with us.

'I suppose the bikes are still OK?' I asked Joe.

'Oui, pas de problème ... I looked at them earlier, still where we left them. Here's the key ... for the padlock. If you want any presents for anybody or anything, il faut le faire cet après-midi.'

'But the shops will still be open this evening,' I said.

'Except we're going to have an early supper and go to bed,' he said.

'Quoi? Joe ...' I started to whine.

He got up from the table.

'No! We've got a long way to go in the morning, so I want to be away at sparrow fart.'

'Quoi,' I screamed, 'qu'est-ce que c'est ... sparrow fart?'

'You've never heard that expression before? Sparrow fart. It means very early. Birds wake up at crack of dawn; presumably it's what sparrows do when they wake up!'

I started giggling. Dominique was laughing too.

'Sparrow fart ... brilliant!'

'Je ne comprends pas ... what is this?' asked Caroline.

'Paul peut t'expliquer ... you'll explain, won't you.'

He was chuckling as he walked away, shouting bon cyclisme and various other things; Dominique got up too.

'A bientôt. Have fun,' she said, 'and be careful.'

Caroline smiled at me. 'Alors, dis-moi.'

'Er ... il est impossible. I have no idea, aucune idée, how ... on peut dire ça en français.'

'Mais il faut que tu essaies ... you must try,' she insisted.

'OK, OK. A small bird, un petit oiseau, a sparrow ... no, I can't.'

'Continue ... cet oiseau, de quelle couleur? Noir, brun?'

'Oui, brun ... mainly brun ... et très petit.'

'OK, peut-être un moineau, et puis ... there was another word.'

'Fart,' I whispered, and of course I went red.

'Je comprends peut-être, c'est un mot grossier, vulgaire?'

'Vulgar, that's right.' I knew I was still bright red, but she was obviously expecting me to go on. I couldn't remember any polite words for it in English. Then I had a bright idea.

I stuck my tongue between my lips and blew a wet raspberry.

'Dans la toilette ...' I started. She screamed with laughter.

'Quoi? Un petit oiseau peut faire ça?'

'Oui, oui, oui!' I'd noticed that the French often repeat oui oui lots of times.

'Early in the morning, les oiseaux, après dormir, they wake up, réveiller ... la première chose, c'est ...' and I blew another raspberry.

'Alors, Joe a dit que ... il faut que nous partons, before ... avant que les oiseaux ...' and I blew one more!

She was now laughing hysterically and I joined in. She leaned over and grabbed my knee.

'Comme tu es ...'

I didn't understand what she said I was, but this time it was obviously a good thing to be!

'Allons-y,' she said, 'let's go.'

'Maybe this is the answer,' I thought to myself. 'Whenever we can't make ourselves understood in words, we do it by noises … noises enfantins!'

9 ... WEDNESDAY AFTERNOON

We walked round to the bikes. I undid the padlock.

'Alors, aujourd'hui, je prends Stumpy et voilà Ghengis pour vous, non non, pour toi.'

She wanted to know why the bikes had names. I tried to explain, as we rode along the road past the war cemetery. There was a short uphill section.

'Merde, comme ça c'est difficile.'

'Qu'est-ce que c'est?' I enquired.

'Les vitesses, the gears, I don't like the ... how you say ... les poussoirs.'

The Saracen was newer than the Specialised and it had trigger gears. Caroline wasn't used to them.

'No worries, we'll swap. Changer?'

'Mais Joe a dit que tu dois prendre Stumpy.'

'He won't mind, he won't even know.'

I changed the saddle heights; Caroline is almost as tall as me but I like having the saddle higher. It makes your legs work better and looks cool!

'On continue?' I suggested.

'Bien sûr.'

We coasted along in brilliant sunshine. The sun was shining, the wind was in our hair, it's lucky I don't write poetry.

As we came to the rougher track leading down through the vineyard, she turned to me.

'Pas trop vite. Doucement, doucement, s'il te plaît.'

That's a great word that Joe had taught me. He said there used to be a police series on television long ago called "Softly, Softly"; he'd wondered if the French version was "Doucement, Doucement".

I led the way gently downhill, but it's odd; when it's quite bumpy, it seems easier to keep going. I went a bit faster. Caroline was immediately behind me; there were no complaints.

I didn't see what happened, I just heard it. There was this horrid clatter, a thump, scraping gravel noise, then nothing. I skidded to a stop, turning to look back. Caroline was flat on her back, not moving. Half the bike was in the hedge. There was now no sound.

I threw my bike on the ground and ran back, perhaps twenty metres.

'Caroline. What happened?'

I looked down at her. Her eyes were wide open. She was winded, sucking desperately for air.

'Doucement,' I whispered. 'Try to take small breaths.'

I put my hand lightly under her head, and held one hand. She winced. I saw blood on my hand. I had never done a first aid course. I had no idea what to do.

She was struggling to sit up. I thought if anything was broken it was a bad idea, but she needed to breathe. She pushed herself up.

'Oh, my God,' I whispered.

The whole of her back was a red raw mass of blood. The back of one ear was bleeding. Her arms, elbows, palms, all were an appalling mess. The bike had dumped her on her back and she'd slid yards along the gravel.

'Mère de dieu. Je pensais que ...'

'Sh..., just breathe quietly.'

I didn't want her to know what a state she was in. I was worried about shock.

'I will go to get help, but you must get in the shade. Can we get you to that tree?'

She nodded yes and put one arm round my shoulder. As gently as possible, I led her staggering to the tree; there was a patch of grass underneath. I lowered her slowly to the ground.

'Oh my God,' she said in English. She had noticed my shirt collar, my neck, both covered with her blood. She looked at the inside of her arms. She started sobbing, desperate cries. They wrenched at me too. I put my hands on her shoulders.

'Rest,' I said, 'je reviens ... cinq minutes maximum.'

Why hadn't I brought my phone with me? Bloody silly doubts about roaming. I had spotted a house about a hundred metres ahead of us. They must have a telephone. I ran down the track. There was a gate and a path leading to the back-door. I was met by a scruffy mongrel. He barked like mad and nipped at my feet.

An elderly lady appeared in the doorway, very Italian. Why do they wear black clothes when it's so hot?

'Buon giorno. Questo ...' and then she saw the blood on my hands, my shirt.

She grabbed my arm and started to pull me inside. She was asking lots of questions in Italian. We were in the kitchen; she pushed me towards the sink and turned on the tap.

'No, no, not me,' I started.

'Accident ... emergency ... my friend ...' The nice lady looked terribly upset, but had no idea what I was on about.

'Telefono ... telefono?' I was fairly sure I'd seen this written on phone boxes. It seemed to work.

'Si, telefono.' She still looked questioningly at me. Try again.

'Ambulance ... hospital ... ambulance ...'

Then something inspired me.

'Ambulanza?' I learned afterwards that I'd guessed the right word. Somebody up there was on my side.

'Si, si, ...' but still she thought it was for me. She started looking at my hands.

'No, no,' I screamed at her. I pulled her to the door and pointed up the track.

'Friend ... ami ... bloody hell ... Caroline ... Caroline ... Carolina ...'

At last she realised what was going on. She was torn between going to see what had happened and doing some telephoning. At my shoving insistence, the telephone won. She shouted into it, long and loud; I didn't understand a word.

She slammed down the receiver and rushed out with me in pursuit. The dog had to come too, yapping furiously with excitement.

Caroline hadn't moved. Tears were rolling down her face, mingling with the blood; she'd wiped her eyes with bloody hands. The effect was awful; it looked as though her face was scratched all over too. There was already a buzzing of flies.

'Paul, il faut aller a l'hôpital. Mais, maman, il faut aller aussi à l'hôtel. '

'Stay quiet. This lady has telephoned. An ambulance is coming.'

'Ambulance?'

'Oui, immédiatement ... non, dans quelques minutes.'

The Italian lady crouched on the ground, dabbing at Caroline's face with her kitchen cloth. She hadn't seen the state of Caroline's back. I felt lost; I had no idea what to say or do.

It was only about five minutes before we heard the waa-waa noise of an ambulance. I saw in the distance a cloud of dust coming towards us. It turned out to be a blue Fiat police car leading a convoy of two ambulances. The old lady must have thought there'd been a massacre. We were quickly surrounded by policemen and four men from the ambulances.

They started to prepare a stretcher then realised she'd be better sitting. The whole of her back and legs were such a mess; her white shorts were torn and not very white any more. Her back was a patchwork of different colours; some cuts were still bleeding, others had dried a dark red-brown. They dabbed at it with tissues and she winced.

One of the policemen started to quiz the old lady. Although she had no idea what had happened, there was a lot of gesticulating; she kept waving at me. He then fired questions at me. I understood no Italian and he didn't know how to ask in English.

It was all quite hectic. At one point even the dog was in the ambulance; they literally kicked him out. They helped Caroline into a sort of wheel-chair and lifted it carefully into the back of one vehicle. I wondered whether I should go with her, but there were the bikes and I'd got to tell Joe and her Mum.

There was nowhere for them to turn round, so they all backed slowly down the track, with all the blue lights flashing and the sirens wailing.

She was gone. I stood in the middle of the track, more helpless than ever. The old lady was saying things like 'mamma mia' over and over.

I pulled Stumpy out of the hedge. The front wheel was buckled and the tyre punctured; that's what had caused the accident. There were sharp stones all down the track, but we hadn't had a problem before.

I half-carried the bike down to where mine was. Signalling to the lady, who was still totally distraught, I put Stumpy just inside her gate, in the garden. She looked happy until I climbed on my bike. She wanted me to stay.

'No, hotel, hotel,' I said. She didn't understand.

'Mama, mama,' I tried; I had to find Caroline's Mum.

I started back up the track, triggering into the lowest gear. As I rode away, I guessed what she was shouting at me ... 'polizia'.

The police were going to escort the ambulance to the hospital and then come back, probably to take a statement from me in Italian! It occurred to me that you can get arrested for leaving the scene of an accident. I changed up a couple of gears and rode harder, to take my mind off Italian prisons. I don't much like spaghetti; that's probably the best thing you'd get, even for Sunday

lunch or on your birthday.   Ugh ... an Italian prison for my
fourteenth birthday! Joe would have to sort it.

10 ... WEDNESDAY LATER

It took me about a quarter of an hour to get back to the hotel. The place seemed dead; it was afternoon sleep time. Luc and Claudia were both sun-bathing by the pool. She sat up and looked at me.

'Wow, what has happened to you?'

Luc sat up too and his mouth literally dropped open.

'Mais, pourquoi ... où est Caroline?'

'Accident. I'll tell you later. I have to find Joe ... or Dominique. Where are they?'

'I haven't seen either since lunch,' said Claudia. They were both still asking questions as I ran away.

Before I reached the door of Joe's room, I could hear Bohemian Rhapsody. It was Queen today, not Mozart.

'Thank God he's there.'

I banged so furiously he must have the thought the place was on fire.

'OK, OK, I'm coming.'

He'd been working on his lap-top. He's always writing and gets quite a lot of stuff published.

'What has happened?'

I started to gabble.

'Paul, come in the bathroom and let's clean you up while you tell me, quickly but intelligibly.'

'Yes, but we must get Dominique too.'

'I expect she's asleep, but OK.'

I heard him go and knock on her door and she appeared almost immediately.

In the tiny scruffy bath-room, I told them the story. Dominique insisted on helping me wash, although I explained there was nothing wrong with me. I pulled off my polo shirt, which was seriously blood-stained, and put it in the basin to soak.

Even before I'd explained why I expected to end up in prison, Joe was on the 'phone to the police. It turned out that Caroline had told them the name of the hotel; there was a police car on its way.

Dominique was in tears; make-up was running down her face.

'Tu es certain que rien n'est cassé? Son visage, il est un peu ... abîmé?'

'No, I think no, but I don't know. She was conscious OK, and somebody at the hospital must speak English ... no ... French. She'll tell them what hurts.'

We heard the police arriving, wailing, and could see the blue light. It looked like an Alfa Romeo.

'Let's go. But Paul, you need to get a clean shirt.'

'That was it, my last,' I told him.

'Borrow one of mine, but you'll look like a clown. It'll be three times your size. And the swimming shorts are going to look ... oh, it doesn't matter.'

'I can grab an evening one, I'll catch you up.'

I ran to my room, dragged on a pair of chinos and the shirt, and caught them up by the police car.

'They want us to go with them, but I'd rather take this so we've got our own transport,' he said, waving at the Discovery.

'OK, OK, seguire! Ma veloce, veloce! ' said the police driver.

Joe told us this meant we had to follow, fast! Italians are probably the most outrageous drivers in Europe, so Italian policemen have to be quicker than their customers. An Italian policeman with the blue light on, in an emergency, a pretty girl's life at stake (well, maybe) and an Englishman trying to keep up, that has to be the ultimate. Joe's driving was really stunning. So of course was George, the Discovery!

We screamed down the main road into Garda, steep and winding, tyres squealing on every corner. Other cars pulled over for the police, but they weren't expecting us, just behind. Joe couldn't afford to get left behind; most Italians pull out fast behind the police to get a clear run through the town. Not in front of us, Joe had decided. He kept right on their tail.

The hospital was probably twenty minutes along the lake. We were all shaking when we got there. There was more Italian conversation. Joe said they wanted Dominique to go in alone. He and I sat outside.

'I can't understand it. The Saracen is almost brand new. Those tyres are meant to stand up to tracks. You're sure it was a puncture?'

'Joe, I'm sorry, it wasn't the Saracen. Caroline was riding Stumpy.'

I explained why. He was very decent and didn't give me a hard time.

'It still doesn't make sense. I put new tyres on Stumpy only a few months ago.'

When Dominique came out, she looked exhausted but was smiling.

'Rien de cassé. Rien de blessé au visage. Merci au bon Dieu. She has lots of pain but all will be OK finally.'

'Can we go in?' I asked.

'Elle veut dormir, on lui a donné du sédatif.'

'Sedative, to calm her, help her sleep,' said Joe.

'Yea, thanks, I'd guessed.'

'We can probably peep through the window?'

'Bien sûr.'

There was almost nothing of Caroline to be seen. I could make out the shape of her feet, then there were enormous hoop arrangements; they must be to keep the sheets off her back. They hid her head too.

We drove back more sedately.

'Tu veux aller visiter encore ce soir?' Joe asked Dominique.

'Merci, non. Ils ont dit qu'elle dorme plusieurs heures. Demain, de bonne heure, ça suffit.'

'Mais vous savez ...'

'Yes, don't worry, I know you must go very early. At the farting of the birds!'

This got rid of some of the tension; we all laughed loudly.

I suddenly realised that I wasn't going to see her again. How unfair, just when things were beginning to click.

We dropped Dominique at the hotel.

'Allons secourir Stumpy,' said Joe. 'Tu penses qu'on peut passer par ce chemin?'

'It's very narrow, but it'll be quicker than going all the way round.'

The hedges brushed both sides as we bumped down to the cottage.

'George enjoys being off-road,' I said.

The dog heard us coming and rushed out on to the track. He barked furiously; he wasn't used to such exciting days.

The bike was still where I'd left it. Joe thought the police might have taken it away. He insisted on going to the door to thank the old lady for all she'd done.

'Le pauvre Stumpy,' he said, as we lifted the bent machine into the car.

When we got back to the hotel, I offered to give Joe a hand with the other bike.

'Non, va chercher les autres. Tout le monde veut savoir ce qui s'est passé. Je vais regarder la roue et son pneu. A bientôt.'

'Pareillement,' I said grinning.

I'd lost track of time. It was still only just after five and the others were on court.

'Hey, Paul, come and join us,' called out Hans.

'Thanks, but no, it's been a bit of a day. It's not worth changing and my kit's all smelly.'

'So, what's new?' asked Hans cheerily.

'Take five,' he said to the others and came over. Claudia understood but Luc looked blank.

'Hans, say it in French,' she suggested.

'Himmel, no idea. A pause, what's the French for pause.'

I looked blank.

'Mais je connais ce mot,' said Luc. 'Les pattes, n'est-ce pas? Pourquoi tu parle des pattes ... il n'y a pas de chien là, je ne vois aucun chat.'

'Wait, wait,' said Hans, laughing. 'Pause, not paws. Of course I'm not talking about cats and dogs.'

'Mais oui, pause, pause, le même mot en français,' said Luc.

'Bien entendu, je suis fou! Alors cinq minutes de pause.'

Everybody laughed but I was sure Luc knew all the time what Hans was saying. He probably understood German as well. He might be a spy later in life.

'So,' said Hans, 'Dominique has told us how Caroline is, but we don't really know what happened.'

'It looks like the front tyre burst. It chucked her on the ground on her back. She had on that swimsuit with hardly any back to it. She was just a total mess. And she couldn't breathe for quite a while.'

'La pauvre Caroline,' said Hans. 'Elle reste à l'hôpital pour plusieurs jours?'

Amazingly I understood.

'We don't know how long she'll have to stay in. On ne sait pas, pour combien de temps, il faut qu'elle reste là.'

We talked a bit more and then Hans insisted on more tennis.

'Join us; it's your last chance. You don't need kit. Swim shorts and shoes, that's all.'

I ran upstairs and got quickly into the swimming shorts I'd been wearing earlier. They had blood on too. It's pretty cool to go and play tennis in kit covered with your girl friend's blood. I stopped for a second; this was the first time I'd thought of Caroline as actually being my girl friend. Wow!

Luc and I played against Claudia and Hans. Luc was now trying hard to be nice; he kept congratulating me on my shots.

After the tennis we all swam. Joe, Dominique and Ilse were there too. The pool gets lots of sunshine at the tail end of the day; it was beautiful. Everybody was more friendly, more relaxed, as though the accident had bound us together.

The evening was much the same; they knew that we had to leave early in the morning for Gran's funeral.

'Paul, tu dois revenir rester chez ton oncle,' said Dominique. 'Tu peux aussi venir au domaine de mon père, le grand-père de Caroline, au lac.'

'I hope he asks me. I'd like to meet the Vicomte again.'

'Tu l'as rencontré dans l'avion, il sera heureux de t'inviter, bien sûr.'

'No, I didn't mean him. What I meant was that I hope Joe asks me again.' I turned to look at him.

'Please, Uncle, you will, won't you.'

'Not if you talk like that, I won't. And next time, I shall ban English completely. On ne parle que français, seulement français.'

'Well, that'll shut me up,' I laughed.

'Bedtime, l'heure du coucher,' said Joe.

'Oui, mon oncle!'

'Alors, je ne t'invite pas!'

'OK, je peux écrire direct au Vicomte, il m'a donné sa carte, j'ai son adresse,' I replied. 'Il va m'inviter … sans doute'

Everybody laughed and then there was a lot of kissing. Dominique gave me a great big hug; her perfume was wonderful but she used even more than I did with Dad's after-shave. Claudia's kiss went on a bit longer than expected. Luc's hand-shake was positively warm.

'Come back next summer,' said Hans.

11 … THURSDAY MORNING EARLY

Joe called me on the room-to-room telephone.

'Voici ton reveil. Six heures du matin ... six o'clock, wakey, wakey.'

'Merci, monsieur. Je suis prêt pour le départ.'

'What happened?' he asked me a few minutes later downstairs. 'Couldn't you sleep?'

'I don't know. It was a bit of a day, yesterday. I was thinking about Caroline quite a lot. And I do have one problem.'

'That sounds bad. Let's just get on our way then you can tell Uncle Joe. It can wait a few minutes?'

I nodded. He had already packed the bikes in, while I'd been playing my last tennis. He did it in a very systematic way, so they didn't rattle. Our bags went behind the bikes.

'Tu n'as rien oublié? Je ne veux pas revenir.'

'More's the pity,' I said. 'No, I haven't forgotten anything. Have you paid?'

'Oui, merci, j'ai payé hier soir ... and had a row. The night we were out to dinner, they charged us for eating in the hotel.'

'But surely,' I said 'they can't do that.'

'They'd got food for us, which they'd paid for. That's their argument. It's a shame ... I might have come here again.'

'Comme ils sont stupides,' I grunted.

'And ...' he went on, 'aller dîner était mon idée, donc je ne peux pas laisser Dominique payer pour un souper qu'ils ne mangeaient pas.'

'You paid the hotel for them too?' I asked in surprise.

'Yes, and I don't entirely trust them. Alors j'en ai parlé à Dominique hier soir. Et ça provoquait une vraie bagarre! A real row!'

We motored on quietly. There was very little traffic to start with.

'Je ne prends pas l'autoroute; il faut que tu peux voir un peu de l'Italie'

'Great, but have we got time?'

'Oui, voilà pourquoi je voulais sortir de bonne heure.'

Joe didn't know the area well. It was all fairly built-up and the traffic quickly got worse. We stopped at a little café for an Italian breakfast. The important thing was for Joe to top up his caffeine levels. In Italy, where espressos were presumably invented, they are minute cups of practically neat caffeine. Joe always orders doppio, which means double.

'I didn't tell you about my big problem,' I reminded him.

'No sorry, tell me. En français.'

'Joe, you are mean. J'ai voulu ... what's "wake up"?'

'Réveiller, se réveiller.'

'Oui, merci. Alors ... j'ai voulu réveiller Dominique avant notre départ, mais ... it was so early that she'd have killed me ... but can we ring from somewhere? I forgot to get their address ... j'ai oublié de demander sa adresse, non son adresse ... à Paris. I want to be able to write ... je veux écrire à Caroline. The only address I've got is her grandfather's and she may not go there now.'

'Tu n'a pas demandé son adresse ... ça c'est fou?' He laughed.

'Yes, I know, stupid but perhaps, Uncle, you ...?' This time he just grinned.

'Brilliant ... yes, of course, you would have got it ... you do fancy Dominique, don't you.'

'Garçon ingrat! Ungrateful boy!'

'Thanks any way. Merci mille fois! Et tu l'aime, n'est-ce pas? It would be good ... I could fly out to see you and we could go off for weekends in Monte Carlo with the two ladies ... it would be good for my French ... Mum and Dad wouldn't need to know you were leading me astray!'

'You'd be the one leading me astray,' he said. 'Qui va payer pour ça?' he asked.

'Mon oncle Joe ... il est riche.' He just laughed.

Back in the car we talked about the last few days.

'I've been thinking,' he said after a while; 'c'est dommage que je n'écris pas des romans, des contes pour jeunes gens.'

'Novels? Why? Surely you could write anything, even for children.'

'There's a good story, here, now, a sort of bilingual story, une histoire bilingue! You meeting all the others, having to talk French, puis l'accident, quelle histoire. Et le grandpère, le Vicomte, quel vrai personnage!'

'Tu peux le faire' I insisted.

'No, I couldn't, I'm not that sort of writer, my stuff is all about investments and finance ... and I'm too old. It needs to be written from your point of view.' He grinned at me, and waited.

'Oh no ... you mean ... no, I couldn't possibly. I'm no good at English and worse at French. Ouf ... and more ouf!' This was out of the question.

'Good, keep reminding me, we are supposed to be speaking French together. Tu peux commencer sur mon ordinateur portable. Non, attends, c'est mieux de dire MacBook. You wouldn't say portable computer, would you? Ou même, on peut dire lap-top.'

It seemed he wasn't going to let go of this brainwave!

'Wouldn't it be best to wait and see what else happens? The story seems to peter out. Boy meets girl, then never sees her again.'

'Parle français,' he shouted. 'Et bien sûr, tu vas la revoir.'

'On verra,' I said, another good expression I'd learned, 'we'll see.'

'And you can always invent,' he went on. 'It can be fiction, after all. You can make me an ugly brute who beats you up. Et Caroline pourrait être encore plus excitant!'

'Pas possible,' I laughed.

'Mais ... Claudia, il faut changer, elle ne doit pas être noire.'

'Pourquoi pas?'

'Because she's not going to be a very nice character in the story, is she.'

'You can not be serious,' I said. 'Why can't I have a nasty black person? Lots of white people are horrid, so some of the black ones must be too.' I thought for a moment.

'Stuff it,' I said. 'Even if it's fiction, I'd put her in just as she is. I'm not going to discriminate.' I was quite proud of this line.

'OK, comme tu veux, mais si ton éditeur veut que tu le changes?'

'Then I won't let my éditeur publish my book,' I said.

From saying I couldn't possibly write a book, I was now talking about "my book". Silly boy, Paul. Then I wondered, did he do that deliberately? When he mentioned Claudia, he knew how I would react. Could he really be that cunning? Had he planned it all, perhaps to get me writing ... and writing French?

I went on thinking about everything that had happened. Of course he hadn't planned for Gran to die and he cannot have planned the accident either.

'Fate's funny, isn't it?' I said.

'Qu'est-ce que tu veux dire?'

'Well, nobody could have guessed we'd have to come back early because of Gran.'

'Nous devons tous mourir, enfin!'

'I know that, but ... the bike accident ... that didn't have to happen.'

'Tu es certain?'

I looked at him.

'What do you mean? It was just bad luck, particularly for Caroline. We'd only just swapped bikes.'

'That's one of the things that got me thinking.'

'Joe, tell me, what?'

'I wouldn't have told you if we'd been staying on, but … je pense que peut-être ce n'était pas un accident. No … I mean it was an accident, but one that had some help!'

I waited for him to go on.

'While you were having your last hit with Hans and the others, I had a good look at Stumpy. I couldn't understand why the tyre would have gone. I rode down on Genghis to look at that track. It wasn't bad enough to pierce a tyre. I'm sure the wheel was OK until it ran into the hedge. There were rocks in there. That was what buckled the wheel and ruined the tyre. '

'But Caroline was already on the ground before that, so what ...?'

'Exactly ... what? I went all over Stumpy really carefully. And I'm fairly sure I found the answer.'

He paused for dramatic effect.

'Continuez, s'il vous plaît.'

'Non, attention ... continue, s'il te plaît ... je suis "tu", n'est-ce pas?'

But then he went on: 'Le frein arrière … the back brake … ne fonctionnait pas. Certaines vis étaient absentes. Some screws were missing.'

'But someone wanted to hurt her? Who would do that?'

The moment I said this, I spotted my mistake.

'Nobody knew she'd ride that bike.'

'Les autres ont probablement entendu quand j'ai dit que je voulais que tu prends Stumpy.'

'Bloody hell, they wanted to kill me.'

'Not kill, old boy. Just cause you a bit of drama. Presque tout le monde qui utilise un vélo sait, si vous avez seulement un frein avant, vous devez être très prudent. Use only the front brake, hard, and you will skid out of control ... possibly go straight over the handlebars.'

'And land on your back,' I said, shaking my head. 'Caroline thought she had both brakes and so, when we came to that first steep bit, bingo ... '

'Je suis presque certain ... '

'It must have been Luc,' I said. 'What a bastard thing to do!'

'Tu as peut-être raison, mais tu ne peux pas en être certain. Claudia might have been jealous or it could have been someone else, hotel staff or some local vandal having a joke.'

'Jokes are meant to be funny,' I said. 'So what did you do?'

He glanced at me. 'Rien, rien du tout,' he said.

'You can't let them get away with it. Surely the police ought to investigate.'

'Paul, in one way you're right, but sometimes things are best left.'

'That can't be right. If you do something dangerous and get found out, you ought to be punished.'

'Yes, but ... je ne peux pas être sûr que le frein a été altéré. Little screws could have fallen out. And ... we had to leave at sparrow fart this morning. And ... je ne voulais pas laisser Stumpy dans un pays étranger; la police l'aurait gardé comme preuve ... kept him as evidence. And it would have been an unpleasant way to end our visit, nasty for Hans and everybody else.'

'Oui, mais ...'

'Et encore une chose, et surtout, la personne qui l'a fait a probablement déjà été punie.'

I looked at him, puzzled.

'Explain, please.'

'Just for the sake of argument, assume it was Luc, or Claudia for that matter. They wanted to cause you grief. They got Caroline instead and caused her serious grief. Ils n'ont probablement pas trop bien dormi la nuit dernière.'

'OK, they didn't sleep well but I still can't accept they should get away with it,' I said. 'I bet it was Luc.'

Traffic built up more and more; it all got slower and slower. After nearly three hours, we finally hit the motorway. It was almost eleven and we still had miles to go in Italy.

'At this rate, I'm going to have to go on the autoroute once we're in Switzerland. I had hoped to go through more of the mountains.'

'Joe,' I said cautiously. 'Can I ask you something?'

'Yes,' he replied guardedly, 'mais il faut parler français.'

'I've been thinking … j'ai commencé a penser. Ouf, coincidence, on peut utiliser le même mot en français? Une coincidence? I tried to pronounce it with a French accent.'

'Oui, bien sûr!'

'C'était vraiment une grande coincidence que … I was sitting …'

'Je m'étais assis ..'

'Oui, je m'étais assis près du grand-père de Caroline dans l'avion Swiss.'

'Oui, vraiment une grande coïncidence,' said Joe but laughing.

'I don't believe you. How well do you know him?'

'Ouf, pas beaucoup.'

'But you also knew Dominique, already.'

'Je n'ai pas compris … en français?' still laughing.

'Dominique est déjà votre … ton amie, girl friend?'

'Mais non, on ne peut pas dire ça, mais oui oui, nous sommes amis.'

'And what Luc said, as a child, I shouldn't have been sitting next to him?'

'Ouf, ça ce n'est pas si grave.'

'You fixed it.' I wasn't really angry but I was sure that things were being hidden from me. I had quite a few things to try and work out. There's a limit to how many coincidences you can live with.

The car had been climbing for ages. We were going back the same way, through the tunnel near the top of the Grand Saint Bernard pass.

'If we're near the border, we may need the passports this time. Shall I dig them out?'

There was a pause. I looked at Joe. He was scowling.

'Sacré bleu, Gott im Himmel, bloody hotel! Bloody bloody stupid people.'

'You don't mean, they've still got them?'

'Oui, bien sûr, à moins qu'ils te les aient donné.'

I shook my head.

'Merde, alors, merde, merde, merde!'

Apparently it is the normal arrangement in Italian hotels. They take your passports when you arrive to take various details. Later they give them back ... sometimes!

'I'll kill them,' said Joe.

12 … THURSDAY AFTERNOON

Joe pulled into a lay-by, just short of the tunnel entrance.

'Dieu merci, je n'ai pas oublié de recharger mon portable.'

We both got out of the car but I stayed well clear while he called the hotel. I'd never seen him so angry. But surely he could explain to the customs, or police, and get us through without papers. They'd understand. If we had to go back to the hotel, we'd never get to Geneva in time.

'Maintenant, je suis encore plus fâché,' he said when he'd finished the call.

'That girl in the reception, who didn't speak when we arrived, it was her. When I told her we'd come all the way here without our passports, she laughed!

'Elle a dit que ce n'était pas sa faute, j'aurait dû me souvenir! I wish to God I spoke better Italian; it's hard to have a really good row if you don't speak the language.

'Je lui ai dit qu'ils doivent trouver quelqu'un qui peut venir là par moto.'

It was on the tip of my tongue to make a joke, but this was not the right moment.

'She said there's no-one else there and she didn't have a motor-bike. Stupid girl!'

'If we go back, we miss the flight?' I asked.

'Bien sûr … même s'ils les envoyaient en moto.'

'Can't you talk us through, Joe? They may not even want to see them.'

'Cela ne vaut pas la peine d'essayer …It's not worth trying. If I could talk our way into Switzerland, which I don't think I could, we've still got to get through Geneva airport. It would take ages while they telephoned all over the place. Non, c'est fait.'

It did cross my mind that to go back was not a total disaster, from my own selfish point of view. Assuming we stayed overnight, I was sure to be able to see Caroline and might have a chance to "interview" Luc.

'Il y a un vol plus tard, mais même ça, nous ne pouvons pas le prendre, il n'y a pas assez de temps. Un jean et un t-shirt ne conviennent pas aux funérailles de ma mère. I have to go to my place on the way to get some clothes. With tomorrow's early flight, we might make it ... depending on all sorts of things. Let me think ... one step at a time.'

Joe turned the car round. We were very low on petrol; he had hoped to cross into Switzerland before filling up. Petrol's cheaper there.

'Merde, alors, plus d'essence aux prix italiens! Je ne me souviens plus à quelle distance se trouve une station-service'

It wasn't too far and it was all downhill so there was no need to panic. We filled up.

'Merde,' said Joe, 'j'ai payé cent euros, plus que huitante livres! It's bad enough in Switzerland. But there it only cost us huitante something.'

'Huitante-trois,' I remembered.

'Bloody hotel!' said Joe.

This became our catch-phrase for the rest of our trip. Whatever went wrong, it was always "bloody hotel". He looked at his watch.

'Le retour à Garda, même si nous prenons toujours l'autoroute, ce sera plus de trois heures.'

Once we hit the motorway, Joe really put his foot down.

'You're taking out your anger on George,' I said.

'Il aime ça. Nous dépassons un peu la limitation de vitesse; c'est cent trente en Italie.'

'One hundred and thirty m.p.h.?'

'Kilomètres, mon ami, not miles.'

'Right, silly me.'

I kept thinking about the bike accident. Could Luc have done that? Did he hate me so much? Because I'd been more successful with Caroline or because I'd beaten him at tennis? If it wasn't him, who else? I tried to put it out of my mind.

'Do you really use those names for the bikes, normally, or is that for my benefit?' I asked.

'No, I use them all the time, Stumpy and Ghengis would be upset to be anonymous.'

'We've got a Vietnamese boy at school called Quan, so we call him Genghis,' I said, 'Genghis Quan!'

'I know some people with a Rottweiler and they've called him Genghis too,' said Joe. 'By the way, you know those Lada jokes?'

'Yea ... what do you call a Lada with twin exhausts ... a wheelbarrow,' I laughed. 'And a convertible Lada?'

'Yes,' said Joe, 'a skip! Mais en français, comment s'appelle un Lada avec un Rottweiler assis en arrière?'

'Ouf, aucune idée.'

He grinned: 'une très belle voiture!'

As often happened with Joe's jokes, it took me a moment to get it.

'What do we do when we get there?' I asked.

'Have a row, of course, bloody hotel!'

'That won't take all night. Will we stay there tonight?'

'Paul, I can guess what's going through your mind. Tu veux rester là, n'est-ce pas? Je ne suis pas certain. Je préférerais revenir chez moi, si possible. If we got away again quickly, we might make my home by midnight. But we'd be shattered.'

'It's up to you, obviously, c'est à toi à décider,' I said quite pleased with my French.

Just in front of the main entrance to the hotel was a police car, blue light going round but nobody inside. Two officers came rushing out as we arrived, with Joe spraying gravel everywhere, deliberately I'm sure, as we crunched to a halt.

As we arrived, Hans was on court with Claudia and Luc, but he came rushing over. The others followed more slowly.

'You tell Hans what's happened,' said Joe. 'I'll go and have the row.'

'Hang on,' said Hans, stopping Joe, 'we've heard. Maria was really upset when you screamed at her on the 'phone. She came to me in tears.'

'I'd like to shout at her again,' said Joe.

'Don't worry. She's gone off duty ... it's Giorgio now and Michele's here. You won't make them cry.'

The two policemen came and introduced themselves. One of them I'd already met; he'd been with the ambulance at the scene of the accident. We were making life a bit exciting for them; they were probably not used to so much activity. There was a lot of 'buongiorno' but otherwise not much understanding until Hans explained.

'Maria called Michele, he owns the hotel, to say she couldn't work here any more because one of the clients had upset her so much. She complained that you had asked her to ride a motor-bike to meet you.'

I wanted to start laughing but Hans went on: 'Luckily I arrived in the middle of this and told Michele that you were not being unfair because you had left for a very serious reason, the unexpected death of your grandmother, and that you are a seriously important person living in Geneva. In Italy that's serious; Grandmas are very respected! And Geneva sounds serious ...'

'Even if I don't live there ...' Joe interrupted.

'It turns out that Carlo here,' Hans waved at one of the policemen, 'is Michele's brother. Because they didn't have your mobile number to contact you, he agreed to come here and escort you back to the border at top speed.'

I looked at the police car, very different from the Alfa we'd followed before. It was a rather old Fiat of some type, bigger than a 500 but not much.

'Well, OK, that's very kind but first where are the passports and I thought Dominique would still be here,' said Joe.

'Alles in Ordnung,' replied Hans, 'passports are with Michele who must still be inside at the desk and Dominique's down by the pool.'

"OK, I need a bathroom. Paul, aller chercher les documents. Thank the boss for the escort, and then we'll go and say hello and goodbye to Dominique.'

As I came back out with the precious documents, Luc stopped me.

'Pas de veine, malchance,' he said. 'How you say ... bad luck.'

I couldn't resist it. 'Oui, merci. Just like the accident, comme l'accident, malchance!'

'Quoi? Qu'est-ce que tu veux dire?' He looked puzzled but he'd gone red too. Guilty conscience?

'Nothing. Excusez-moi. Rien.'

Hans had overheard this and said quickly to Luc and Claudia : 'You two have a hit for a few minutes.'

Luc stood watching as Hans and I went down the steps.

'What was that about?'

'It's best if Joe tells you.'

'But ...'

Joe appeared.

'You've got them?' I nodded.

'Ouf … maintenant, on peut quitter l'Italie … legally. With police assistance!'

'You must have been very aggressive on the phone,' said Hans.

'You don't know me very well,' replied Joe, 'I'm the gentlest creature.'

'That's not the impression Maria had on the 'phone; we're probably going to be looking for a new receptionist.'

'Hans, I'm sure she misunderstood. My Italian's not very good. I certainly didn't want her to ride a motor-bike. We'd never have seen our passports again!'

I spluttered with laughter.

'Dominique's down by the pool,' said Joe. 'She can tell you how the patient is.'

I'd been here several minutes and I hadn't asked anyone yet about Caroline. Dominique was sitting on a sun-bed under an umbrella. She was talking to someone I didn't recognise from the back.

She jumped up. 'Joe, Paul, c'est bon de vous revoir, mais je suis désolé de vos problèmes.'

She waved a hand at the visitor, who was also getting to his feet. He turned round.

'Joe, je veux présenter mon père, le Vicomte de Launay de St.Etienne. Papa, tu connais Paul. Ce Monsieur est Joe Walters, l'oncle de Paul.'

'Monsieur, bonjour.'

Joe turned to Dominique : 'Il n'y a pas besoin de maintenir la prétention, merci; Paul sait que nous nous avons déjà rencontré.'

The large bearded gentleman looked just the same as on the aircraft, grossly overdressed for the weather. He extended a hand towards Joe.

'Enchanté, Monsieur, de vous revoir.'

He turned to shake my hand too.

'Et Paul, tout va bien? All goes well.'

'Oui , Monsieur. Merci beaucoup. Tout va bien pour moi, mais ... pas pour Caroline.'

This was good, even more French from me. I turned to Dominique.

'How is she today? Have you been to see her?'

'Mais Paul, tu parles français avec mon père et anglais avec moi. Pourquoi?'

'My French isn't good enough for important questions.'

'But Caroline has told me. She speaks to you in French. Alors, aujourd'hui, elle va beaucoup mieux, merci. Hier c'était trop douloureux ; il fallait nettoyer toutes ses blessures. Il y avait du sable, des petits gravillons enfoncés dans son dos, dans ses jambes.'

'Help! I hardly understood. She's better today and what else?'

Her grandfather came to my aid.

'They must clean her back. There were many little stones and sand in her wounds.'

He said "wounds" like "pounds".

'That's awful. It must have been painful.'

'My father has come here immediately when he heard about the accident. We are going to see her again soon. Il faut nous accompagner. You must come.'

I looked at Joe.

'Perhaps. I need to make some telephone calls. To your father, Paul, and Swiss International Airlines for starters. But I said to that man in there' ... he waved towards the hotel ... 'I said it would be easier to use their office telephone because my phone doesn't get a very good signal here. Il a refusé. Il a dit que je devais payer. Alors, j'ai refusé'

Le Vicomte put his hand in his pocket and pulled out the same super-looking mobile phone which I'd seen on the flight.

'S'il vous plaît,' he said.

'C'est très gentil mais …' said Joe.

'Mais non, j'insiste.'

'Thank you, the numbers I need are in the car. And I must talk to my escort, I cannot keep the carabinieri waiting for ever!' He walked away.

'I must go back to my tennis players, but we still have a conversation to finish, before you go anywhere,' said Hans turning to me.

I just nodded. Dominique spoke quickly to her father in French.

'Bien sûr,' he replied. 'Paul, va vite vers ton oncle. Tu es invité de revenir demain avec nous dans mon château.'

Invité was the key word, and château, I understood those.

'Merci, merci beaucoup.' I ran to the car. Joe was talking on the mobile. I waved furiously.

'Your son is waving at me ... hang on a minute.'

I explained that they'd asked me to go with them.

'Judith, I'll have to ring you again in a few minutes. Don't go away.'

We walked back to the others together. Hans and Dominique were talking, Luc and Claudia still on court. Joe explained that Swiss International only had one seat left on the early flight tomorrow. For him to catch that flight meant driving tonight and starting from his home very early tomorrow.

It seemed too good to be true. I waited for him to reach the right conclusion.

'Caroline peut voyager demain, retourner dans votre château?' he asked.

'Oui, dans la Mercedes de mon père,' Dominique replied. 'Sans problème.'

I hadn't noticed the car before. It was parked along past the main door of the hotel, in the shade under the trees. It was a very sleek black BMW. A chauffeur was standing beside it.

'Paul, you're happy to stay on your own?'

'Of course, but I won't be on my own,' I answered.

'Good,' said Dominique, 'and now I don't drive alone. Mon père ne veut pas rouler dans ma voiture. Il dit que je roule trop vite.'

This made Joe look nervous but he didn't say anything. A few minutes later it was all fixed. Joe would go home immediately to

Switzerland and fly to London for the funeral. He would fly back on Saturday morning and come to the château for lunch to pick me up.

'Super,' said Dominique.

'But wait,' said Hans, 'Paul has no bed for tonight. Michele has already rented your two rooms to some new people, les deux chambres sont déjà louées.'

I was going up and down like a yo-yo. One minute it all looked great, the next not.

'Pas de problème,' said Dominique. For a moment I was nervous; I thought she was going to offer me Caroline's bed in their double room!

'Nous pouvons ... excusez-moi ... in English ... we can arrange a room for him at the hotel, where my father is staying ... it is very grand.'

Claudia had just joined us and was listening to the conversation. Luc was nowhere to be seen.

'Luc a une chambre à deux lits,' she said; 'Paul peut se coucher là!'

'Je ne suis pas certain que ce soit une bonne idée,' said Dominique.

'Why not?' said Joe. 'Paul won't mind and it'll certainly be cheaper.'

I understood this too. I could share with Luc. I preferred the idea of staying in the grand hotel with the Vicomte but I knew that I had to agree.

'It's OK by me.'

'Comme vous voulez,' said Dominique, a bit unhappily. I wondered why.

Sharing with Luc, would I be safe? Would he be safe?

13 ... THURSDAY EVENING

Once everything was agreed, Joe made a couple more telephone calls. Then he asked me how many euros I had left.

'Il n'aura pas besoin d'argent,' said Dominique.

'Oui mais, à tout hasard, just in case'.

I'd hardly spent anything but he gave me more euros. I'd never felt so rich.

'Merci, Joe, merci beaucoup!'

Then quietly he told me to behave myself with Caroline, Luc and everyone else, and have fun ... and think about 'my book'!

'Of course I will, Joe, and thanks for everything.'

The two policeman had been quietly smoking all this time and talking to the owner. They seemed to be in no hurry.

Joe called out to them 'andiamo, let's go!' They wandered slowly to their car; this was supposed to be an escort to get him to the border as fast as possible.

'Excusez -moi, il faut que je prends ma portable.'

Joe looked at the Vicomte. 'Ouf, je suis vraiment désolé. Comme je suis fou.'

He handed the phone back. 'That's so embarrassing. Merci mille fois!'

Joe gave Dominique a kiss but just in the formal way that French people seem to kiss each other all the time.

'Trois fois,' he said, 'three kisses, c'est normal en Suisse, à Paris c'est quatre, n'est-ce pas?'

He shook my hand vigorously.

'Au revoir. And please say goodbye to Ilse and Luc for me' he said to Hans and Claudia.

There was no scrunching of the gravel as the little Fiat led George, the big Discovery, out of the drive. We all waved.

'I think Joe will get very frustrated,' I said and looked forward to hearing later how he'd got on.

'Je reviens à mon hôtel,' said the Vicomte to Dominique, 'et vous êtes tous invités, ce soir, n'est-ce pas?'

We were all to have dinner with the Vicomte, Claudia and Luc as well as me. Hans said Ilse was not feeling very well and so he would stay to keep her company.

Claudia had told Luc I'd be sharing his room for the one night. He didn't seem to mind and led me upstairs. His room was a bit bigger than mine. The two beds were longways so we didn't have to sleep side by side which was good news. He seemed to be living out of his bag, but I did the same, never really unpacking.

Before we went out, I had to sort out my kit. Having been shut up for several hours in the steaming hot car, it was almost crying to be let out.

'Il faut laver tout ça,' I said pulling all the used tennis kit out of the bag. He grinned and held his nose.

'Oui, dans la douche.' He reached in to turn on the water. Why was he being so helpful?

I stripped off, and took a whole heap of kit in with me. His bathroom was better than mine had been, it had its own toilet. Luc produced a tube of detergent and handed it in. I overdid it a bit; in no time the whole shower was full of lather. By the time I'd finished rinsing the clothes and myself, the water was stone cold. I explained to Luc.

'Hot water, l'eau chaud, c'est fini. That means cold showers for everyone and they'll complain to the hotel.'

We both laughed. He'd understood every word, in English.

'You understand English, don't you?'

'Not always, but pretty good.'

'Why pretend not to?'

'It is good when people think I don't understand. At school they say you English, you expect always that we speak your language. It is true.'

For the moment the friendly Luc had faded again; he seemed a really moody guy. I thought I'd try a subtle approach; he had agreed I could share his room.

'Merci pour ... le lit ... c'est très gentil ... tu permets que j'occupe ta chambre.'

'Je n'avais pas de choix. They did not ask, they command me.'

He switched on the television then lay on his bed.

'Merde, pas ça!' There was no remote control. He got up and flicked through the channels until he came to MTV. He lay back and lit a cigarette.

'Ça, c'est mieux.'

I wanted to talk to him about the accident. But if he was guilty, I thought, he'd probably raise the subject. This was cunning of me but maybe he was too cunning?

'Au sujet de l'accident ...' I started.

'Quel accident?' Big mistake, he was guilty! I laughed.

'How many have there been? L'accident de Caroline, n'est-ce pas?'

'Oui, je me suis trompé. I made the mistake.'

'Quoi? Quoi?' I screamed. I'd thought he was guilty but ...

'Remettes-toi! Please calm yourself. I explain. J'étais envieux, jaloux, comment dit-on en anglais? You say jealous?' I nodded.

'Il faut comprendre ... je ne suis pas venu ici pour le tennis, mais pour Caroline.'

He hesitated. He said he'd come here specially for her; I wondered if he was making it up as he went along.

'Je l'ai rencontré à Paris, il y a trois quatre mois, à un tournoi de tennis. Et ...'

'Wait. It's important I get this right. You met her in Paris?'

'Yes. At a tournament. Since three or four months.'

'Three or four months ago.' I kicked myself; there was no need to correct his English at this stage.

'I found from a friend her number, telephone. I leave many messages ... elle ne veut pas parler avec moi. Je ne sais pas pourquoi. Puis un ami m'a dit ... he tells me, she comes to play tennis here in Italy. I persuade my father it is good for me to come. He is rich, he can pay. Avant ton arrivée, Caroline était très fâchée contre moi.'

'Quoi. I didn't get that.'

'She was angry. Elle a devinée ... to guess ... she has guessed that I have arranged to come only to see her.'

'So because of that, because she doesn't want to have anything to do with you, you want to kill me?' I was almost shouting.

'Kill? Why you say kill? Il n'y a personne mort. Who dies? Jamais, jamais, I cannot kill.'

'You mucked about with the brakes.'

'Quoi? What?'

' ... mucked about ... tampered ... merde, qu'est-ce que c'est en français? The brakes ... les freins du vélo ...'

He hung his head.

'Oui, je les ai touché,' he said softly. 'Mais je ne voulais pas tuer quelqu'un. Not kill!' The last words were said with enormous emphasis. This boy's disturbed, I thought!

'You didn't want to kill anyone, that's OK then,' I said. He could see the sarcasm on my face, hear it in my voice. He shrugged.

'But you wanted someone to get hurt, maybe badly injured?'

'Mais, non, comme tu grandis ça. You exaggerate that. You have only one brake. That is not so important.'

By now I was really angry. I'd already stood up and moved closer to his bed. I was shaking. I've never hit anyone in my life, not in anger.

'You want to hurt me, kill me?' he barely whispered. He looked up at me but quickly looked away. Suddenly he cracked. His whole body shook with sobs. He was in agony.

I wanted to be sick. I was still furious with him and disgusted and yet, in a way, I felt sorry for him too. He wasn't just crying because he was scared of me.

I went and sat on my bed. For several minutes he was crying into his pillow. I watched the television but without concentrating. How could he have got himself in such a twisted state?

'You've got to talk about it,' I said, 'il faut parler de ça.'

In a mixture of French and English we talked. He insisted he hadn't wanted to hurt anybody, just cause me some grief. He knew I was to ride Stumpy. He kept saying that God had got his revenge by fixing that Caroline had the accident. I'm sure he believed every word of what he said. He was one of those guys who could talk himself into anything.

What was I going to tell the others? Hans already knew I was suspicious. And Luc ought to be punished for what he'd done. But I remembered what Joe had said in the car. Whoever was guilty was already in agony. It looked as though Joe was right. There was one thing I did need to know.

'Did Claudia help you? You two seem to have got more friendly.'

'Claudia? Mais non. Elle ne parle pas beaucoup de français. J'ai expliqué ... I say to her ... qu'est-ce que c'est que j'ai fait ... what I did. She say ... je suis fou, tout-à-fait fou ... you know ... crazy. I not like that. Je ne suis pas fou. She want to say to you, what I want to do. I said no.' His English was getting worse and he'd started to cry again.

I looked at my watch.

'Il est presque sept heures. We need to get ready. Il faut s'habiller pour le diner. Et nous faisons une visite à Caroline.'

'Non, je ne viens pas.'

I thought quickly. I'd have liked him not to come but that made more of a drama out of the whole thing. I'd have to explain his absence. And I still didn't trust him. I'd prefer him to be where I could keep an eye on him. Tomorrow we were leaving any way.

'You have to come,' I said; 'c'est absolument nécessaire. Go and wash your face.'

He didn't try to argue. We both got ready quickly. I still had some unused shirts for evenings.

As we walked downstairs, I said to him: 'It is necessary that you have dinner with us. It is rude to refuse. It is not necessary for you to visit Caroline. I think we are going there first. Tu comprends?'

'Oui, d'accord.'

It looked as though he would do whatever I told him.

The others were waiting for us. Le Vicomte had not come back in the BMW but had sent a taxi. The BMW would not have been big enough for six people. I was invited to sit in the front with the driver. I worried about missing some of the conversation in the back but Dominique seemed to be chatting in a relaxed way with Luc and Claudia.

It occurred to me that you are supposed to take flowers to people in hospital when you visit. But I hadn't had much opportunity and it was too late now.

Hey, this was the big chance when I needed to use my phrase-book. I could even remember the question :

'S'il vous plaît pouvez-vous me dire où se trouve la boutique de fleuriste la plus proche.'

But of course we were in Italy so they probably wouldn't understand any way.

When we got to the hospital Claudia and Luc waited outside. Dominique went in alone to see Caroline. Le Vicomte arrived and we chatted about tennis.

'Tu as joué depuis quel age?' he asked.

'Oh, je suis pas certain, peut-être six ou sept ans.'

'Avec ta famille?'

'Oui, mon père.'

'Et tu as des frères ou des soeurs?'

'Oui, mais plus jeune, ma soeur Sophie a sept ans et Richard a dix ans.'

'Alors tu es le fils aîné.'

I though I'd been doing pretty well until now but …

'Quoi?'

'Fils is son, aîné means oldest, you are the number one son!'

'Ah yes, I guess so … d'accord' I laughed.

When Dominique returned she said 'Caroline est très fatiguée.'

'Elle veut voir seulement Paul. She wishes to thank you for caring for her at the accident.'

This was good news; I needn't have bothered to ban Luc. But the Vicomte complained.

'She wishes to see her young man, not her grandfather!'

'Tais-toi, Papa,' said Dominique. They both laughed. Dominique led the way to the private room.

'Là,' she said, outside the door. 'Ne reste plus de cinq minutes. Maximum five minutes. Il faut qu'elle dors.'

'D'accord. Je comprends.'

I knocked gently on the door as her Mum walked away. There was no answer. The little glass window had a cover which was shut; I couldn't see in. I pushed the door gently open.

'Caroline,' I said quietly. 'C'est moi, Paul.' I pronounced my name the French way.

'Viens, Paul.'

I hesitated. The hoop arrangements that had protected her yesterday had been taken away. Nothing had been put in their place; I mean nothing. I was transfixed. Her legs and back were a mass of cuts and grazes. The hospital must have used some sort of coloured antiseptic; there were lots of orange blotches.

'Excuse me that I am naked,' she said, 'I hope you don't mind.' She was lying on her tummy but with her face turned towards me. I couldn't think of a reply.

'The doctors ... they say it is good to have the air, to leave the wounds not covered.'

'Yes, I understand,' I stuttered, 'je comprends.'

'Mais Paul, tu es embarrassé. Pourquoi? Tu as une soeur. You have seen your sister without clothes.'

'Sophie is only seven. And sisters are different! It's ... it's nothing.'

'In the summer, we go always to the Mediterranean, parfois à une plage naturiste. Pour nous c'est normal.'

I had noticed she didn't have a white tide-mark like most sunbathers. But, I suddenly thought, we were going to stay together at her grandfather's château; I knew he had a swimming-pool. Did this mean I would have to swim naked? No way, I couldn't. I'd have to make an excuse, extremely severe foot rot or something. That would keep me out of the pool, but ... sun-bathing? Fool, think of something better, much more serious, skin cancer?

'J'ai voulu te remercier pour tous que tu as fait. Viens plus proche.'

I moved closer. She grabbed my hand and touched it to her lips.

'Now you must go. Tomorrow morning we go all to the château. And we have much to talk about ... Joe has proposed the writing? I look forward.'

I started to stutter something but no, I leant down and kissed her cheek.

'Au revoir, Caroline.'

'A bientôt, Paul.' She blew a kiss, like she had from her bedroom window.

I suddenly thought 'what irony'! Our English teacher had spent ages giving us examples of irony last term. Only a couple of days ago I'd been embarrassed at being half-naked meeting Caroline in the passage in the hotel and then, too, there was the photo Hans had taken. Now I'd spent time with her, tout-à-fait nue! I must have gone really bright red, she knew I was embarrassed. And I couldn't help wondering what would have happened if the accident had caused her to fall not on her back but on her front. Surely she would not have been naked then. No way was I going to join in for any nudity!

The others were all outside waiting for me. The Vicomte squeezed into the taxi with us and we drove to the hotel where he was staying. It turned out to be the same place that the four of us had had dinner together; it seemed like ages ago. I wondered where the BMW had gone.

We all started looking at the menu which was of course in Italian. Luc had recovered a bit from his gloom.

'Ouf, les prix sont extraordinaires. Est-ce qu'il y a un menu?'

'Non monsieur, seulement à midi,' replied the waiter with what sounded to me like a very good accent.

'The menu …' I started to ask but Dominique helped me out.

'In French a menu is a set meal. It is cheaper than choosing separate dishes, as they say, à la carte. What you hold is not a menu, it's la carte.'

'And in English, a cart is what you have with a donkey!'

Claudia had been very quiet until now and we all laughed.

'Tu as déjà mangé là,' Luc said to me. 'I think that you recommend the carpaccio. En français on dit la viande est crue.'

I'd already discussed it with Mum and she'd been worried about it but I didn't tell Luc that I knew. We all chose it and I was boring enough to have the chicken again.

I was sitting across the table from the Vicomte.

'Alors, Paul, qu'est-ce que tu va faire comme carrière? Tu as décidé ou tu as des idées?'

The word carrière was enough of a giveaway.

'Ouf,' I replied which was a good start.

'Tu as quel âge ?

'I'm fourteen, almost, so I have four more years at school. Then probably university.'

'Oui, entendu, mais tu as des idées, you have some ideas.'

'My father is an engineer …'

'Ah, ingenieur, comme moi mais, moi, j'ai eu plusieurs carrières. Et ton oncle, il est écrivain, n'est-ce pas?'

Ecrire means to write so that was clear enough.

'Yes, he has suggested …'

'En français, s'il te plaît, afin que les autres puissent comprendre.'

Luc opened his mouth, I'm sure to say that he understood English, but sensibly closed it again.

'Ah oui, Joe, mon oncle, il a suggéré, proposé que … je peux écrire aussi.'

'Bon mais quoi, roman, contes … a novel, some stories ou des choses techniques comme lui?'

'Oh, a crazy idea, to write about you, all of us.'

'So I shall be in your book. Ouf. Dis m'en plus … how you do that.'

'Aucune idée,' I was starting to wish I hadn't mentioned it.

Dominique kindly spotted that I was in difficulty and helped me out by changing the subject.

'On peut fixer notre agenda pour demain?'

Back in what was now our room, Luc's room, the earlier conversation seemed to have been forgotten. It was late and we both quickly got ready for bed. I went to brush my teeth.

'Tu n'as pas un pyjama?' he asked when I came out of the little bathroom. I always just wear boxer shorts in bed. He was already wearing pyjamas with long sleeves and legs. I had to spend a night in hospital not long ago and they said I had to take pyjamas but I didn't have any.

Oddly one of the few things I remembered from French lessons at school is that they use the singular word and we talk about pyjamas plural. And the Americans spell the word pajamas. Really useful stuff you learn at school, isn't it!

'Mais non, it's too hot … il fait trop chaud. Je ne porte pas un pyjama même chez moi en Angleterre.'

'Tu veux regarder la télévision?' he asked.

'Merci, non.'

'Excuse me … I have … encore une … the last one.'

I lay on my back in the dark, watching the glow of his cigarette. There was no point in telling him that smoking was strictly forbidden throughout the hotel. I know that some places make a charge to fumigate the room if they discover someone's been smoking.

Our talk had reminded me of Caroline's lack of clothing. I wondered what she would normally wear in bed.

'Je t'envie,' he said.

'Quoi? You do what … to me?'

'Envie … le même mot … envy. I have envy to you.'

'Right, you envy me. Why?'

'I think you are lucky. Perhaps you are happy chez toi, in your house.'

'Yes, most of the time.'

I didn't know if he was just feeling sorry for himself or if life really was tough. Whatever, it was no excuse.

'Let's talk tomorrow. I need sleep. On peut parler demain, n'est-ce pas?'

'D'accord, OK, and … Paul, I am very sorry, vraiment.'

I really wanted to go to sleep but there were so many things going through my mind that I lay awake for quite a while. As well as issues with Luc and the accident, I was really bugged by what seemed to be too many coincidences. Sitting next to Caroline's grandfather on the flight was a big one, made more odd by the story that young people travelling alone are supposed to sit together, not with old men. And Joe already knew him, probably much better than he'd said.

And then the writing idea, the Vicomte had mentioned about Uncle Joe being a writer; did he already know what Joe had suggested to me about writing? And Caroline too, she'd asked 'your uncle has proposed the writing?' It's an odd feeling not to be able to trust Joe completely. Why would he keep that a secret?

Finally, to the sound of Luc snoring and me being kind enough not to shout at him, I fell asleep through sheer exhaustion which, at my age, makes me sound like an old fart.

14 ... FRIDAY MORNING

'Tu veux nager? Swim?' I was barely awake; Luc was standing next to my bed, wearing swimming shorts. I had survived the night, sharing his room! I looked at my alarm clock, it was only seven-thirty.

'C'est trop tôt pour toi, too early?'

'Non, it's OK, nager, une bonne idée.' I got out of bed, pulled on swimming shorts and grabbed a towel.

'Tu avais raison. J'ai trouvé l'air trop chaud dans mon pyjama!

'Tu vas partir à quelle heure?'

'I don't know but not before about nine-thirty I guess. Environ neuf heures et demi.'

As the door was closing, Luc stuck his foot in the way.

'J'ai oublié la clef, the key.' I laughed to myself, remembering my first embarrassment with Caroline.

'What's the French for drown?' I asked him, as we went down to the pool.

'Quoi? Drown. Je ne sais pas. What is drown? Explain please.'

'Merde ... je ne sais pas, mourir, dans l'eau. On ne peut pas, breathe, respirer dans l'eau, au dessous de l'eau. So you die.'

'OK, je comprends. Noyer. Se noyer. Si on ne peut pas nager, on peut se noyer dans la mer.'

'Et, si je veux que tu te noie, on peut dire quoi? Faire noyer?'

'Quoi? Tu veux me tuer maintenant? Mais oui, on peut noyer quelqu'un. Tu peux me noyer.'

'Bon. Merci,' I laughed. 'It was the key that reminded me. You invented a name for me.'

He looked totally blank.

'Monsieur Merde Carrée! You invented that. Tu as inventé ce nom. On peut dire inventer?'

'Ah, mais oui, c'était un bon nom. That is the reason for to drown me?'

'That's one reason!' We both laughed.

I was amazed at myself. This was the guy who'd caused the accident and now we were laughing together. I was relieved that I'd be leaving soon. I suddenly realised I didn't know if he'd been invited to the château as well. I got the answer without having to ask him directly.

'When do you leave here?'

'Demain. We all go tomorrow. Hans and Ilse take us to Milano to the airport. Claudia goes to Frankfurt, I to Paris. But you go today, n'est-ce pas, avec Dominique et son père?'

'Oui.' I almost felt I had to apologise. 'It's a shame, c'est dommage, on n'a pas joué beaucoup de tennis.'

'Non, exact, et pour demain il n'y a que Claudia et moi. Ça, ce n'est pas très intéressant. To play only singles with Claudia.'

'Come on, she's OK.'

'Ouf ... elle a dit qu'elle préfère jouer seulement avec les filles. Peut-être qu'elle est gay!'

'Pour moi, elle est trop jeune pour décider ça,' I laughed.

We were just at the bottom of the stairs, I stopped.

'Hey, pourquoi pas une manche de tennis now, immédiatement, et puis la piscine.'

He stuck his hand out for me to slap. We ran back upstairs and I quickly found some now fairly clean and almost dry kit.

We hit balls for a few minutes and then had one really good set. If anything we were both calling balls in favour of the other guy. I won 6/4 but it could easily have gone the other way. At one point I could see Hans watching us from quite far away but he had the good sense not to interrupt.

'Alors, vite à la piscine,' called Luc.

'Oui, bien sûr, mais avant ça la douche obligatoire!'

There were two showers right next to the pool where I had rinsed out my red wine.

'Oui, OK, d'accord.' We both just stripped off our shirts, showered and dived straight into the pool.

After we'd swum several lengths, we went back up to the room.

'You go in the shower first, if you like,' I suggested. 'I must finish my packing. I'm not exactly sure when we're leaving.'

'D'accord, OK.'

'C'est à toi, maintenant,' he said as he emerged still dripping from the bathroom.

'C'est ton tour, in English you say your turn?'

'Bien sûr.'

'Hey, il n'y a pas besoin de laisser ton chocolat là, merci.'

He was in a really cheerful mood now so I was happy to laugh at his joke. Once I'd closed the bathroom door I made some loud farting noises but I couldn't tell if he heard or not.

Everybody appeared for breakfast.

'Tu es prêt à partir?' Dominique asked me.

'Oui. I've already packed.'

'I go first to prepare Caroline. Tu peux venir avec mon père. Il va arriver à onze heures, toujours à l'heure, exact.'

'I'll be waiting. Je serai prêt à partir.'

'En français, parfait,' she replied.

We all waved goodbye as she managed to churn up some more gravel, which reminded me that I would be keeping her company on the way back to Grandpa's château.

I wanted to avoid talking to Hans because he might have overheard me suggesting to Luc that the accident wasn't an accident. I failed, he grabbed me by the arm and walked me away from Claudia and Luc.

'What were you saying to Luc? You told me to ask Joe but I didn't have a chance.'

'Ouf, Hans, c'était vraiment rien.' It was cool to speak French and bought me thinking time. 'I promise it was nothing to do with tennis and I saw you watching us this morning, best of friends, des bons amis, n'est-ce pas?'

'Mais …'

'Hans, trust me, if there's more to tell you, I shall see you at home next month. Let me go and say goodbye to the others. And say ciao to Ilse for me.'

I thought to myself that was probably OK, 'I think I got away with it'. That's a line from something famous on television but I couldn't remember what, probably Fawlty Towers.

One other thing I noticed : I'd said 'c'était vraiment rien', not 'ce n'était vraiment rien', sort of automatically. I realised that in conversation they don't use the 'ne' thing and I'd picked up the habit.

'Hey, Claudia, almost time to say good-bye.'

'Just when we were getting to know each other,' she said with a smile but a hint of sarcasm. Perhaps I should have spent more time with her but I'd been a bit preoccupied, one way and another, with Caroline and Luc. She offered a kiss but I said 'not yet, I have to get my bag and then you can wave to me as I set off in my limo!'

Luc was already upstairs in our room. He looked as though he'd switched into his gloomy mood. I threw the last few bits into my bag.

'I'm sure you will see Caroline in Paris. You will have a chance to apologise.'

'Mais non. Ça c'est impossible. I hope that I never see her again. I think it is not necessary to tell her, about les freins, the brakes.'

'Luc, c'est à moi de décider, n'est-ce pas?'

'Oui, c'est vrai, mais, j'ai pensé, peut-être ...' He was beginning to whine.

'C'est à moi de décider, n'est-ce pas?'

'Oui, bien sûr,' he agreed. He looked miserable but I didn't want to leave with him thinking me a total 'morceau de merde' so I said : 'We'll meet again some time I'm sure, peut-être un rencontre à Roland Garros ou Wimbledon.'

'Ouf, OK, comme tu as dit, bien sûr. C'est bizarre que tu commence maintenant, au départ, à parler plus français qu'anglais.'

Without warning, he stepped towards me and gave me a hug. It took me a moment to respond. He'd said he thought Claudia was gay and I was going to make a joke about us two. Uncle Joe had told me long ago that British humour is not always understood by foreigners, so I desisted … hey, a good English word for me!

Back downstairs, well before eleven, they were all there to see me off. A black Mercedes rolled across the gravel on the dot of eleven o'clock. There was a lot more kissing and Hans reminded me when coaching would start again in England, once we were home.

Le Vicomte emerged from the front of the car; he had been keeping the chauffeur company. I remembered the chauffeur, the same guy who'd met him at the airport. He looked quite young for such a large car. But this was not the BMW and not yesterday's driver. How many people work for the Vicomte?

'Bonjour, good morning, tout va bien? Tu es prêt?' asked the Vicomte.

'Oui merci, bonjour.'

He suggested we both sit in the back. The car had been got specially ready for Caroline with extra cushions and surely unnecessary blankets. I could not believe that she was going to travel as undressed as yesterday. A truck driver looking down from his cab might have a heart attack, cause an enormous smash!

On the way down to the hospital I thanked Caroline's grandfather again for dinner the night before. 'De rien,' he said. 'C'était mon plaisir.'

'Mes excuses, Monsieur, c'est pas très poli, mais vous avez combien de voitures?'

'Ouf, je ne suis pas certain, mais la voiture que j'ai utilisé hier, la BMW, était louée … it was rented. I must make a fast decision after Dominique tells me Caroline was hurt. Et Jean-Pierre était déjà absent, ailleurs,' he waved towards today's driver. 'Ailleurs … I think you say he was elsewhere. Today we need this car for maximum comfort, pour Caroline, n'est-ce pas? Et pour un tel voyage, si important, je préfère Jean-Pierre comme conducteur.'

At this point I caught him glancing in his mirror. He saw me and smiled.

'A quelle heure tu as quitté le château ce matin?' … more loudly.

'Un peu avant cinq heures, Monsieur,' replied Jean-Pierre.

'J'espère que tu es allé te coucher assez tôt et tu as bien dormi.'

'Oui oui Monsieur, merci.'

This I understood easily; the Vicomte was concerned that our driver wasn't going to be too tired to drive but the poor guy had been up since before five! And I was confused by something else. The Vicomte was saying "tu" but Jean-Pierre was replying "Monsieur" in a very respectful way.

At the hospital they were already outside in the sun. Caroline was standing talking to one of the doctors. I was relieved to see she was dressed this time, wearing a very loose white dress which looked way too big for her. It was probably one of her mother's; I guessed it was the only way she could be comfortable.

'Ne te moque pas de moi, ça n'a rien de drôle.' I vaguely remembered that there was an old song "Don't Laugh at Me".

'Mais non,' I grinned, 'très élégant'. She stuck her tongue out.

'Caroline, ça n'est pas poli,' said Dominque.

'Bon, je ne voulais pas faire un geste poli!'

Her grandfather kissed her on both cheeks and asked how she was. I did the same and I got quite an enthusiastic response. Then she was helped into the back of the Mercedes. I had to keep Dominique company. Her little Peugeot must have had GTi and turbo and other messages on the back. She drove flat out the whole way.

We talked a bit in a mixture of French and English. I recognised quite a lot of the motorway; I had now driven it three times with Joe. But she wasn't aiming for the same pass with the Saint Bernard dogs. We crossed the frontier into France by the Mont Blanc route which means going through a very long tunnel.

'Il y a eu un accident épouvantable ici, il y a quelques années,' she told me, while we were rolling through in a queue of mainly trucks.

'Vraiment terrible, un camion a pris feu, il y a eu beaucoup de morts. You understand? Camion ... a truck, burning.'

'Wow,' I thought, 'what an appalling way to die,' but I would have preferred to have been told later.

'Oui, affreux!' was all I could think of to say.

After the tunnel, Dominique had to stop for petrol and I was amazed; the Mercedes pulled in almost immediately behind us.

Her father and I both got out of the cars and I heard him insist on paying for her petrol.

'Ce n'est pas nécessaire, mais si tu insistes, merci beaucoup.'

'Et, Dominique, pourquoi pas si vite que la normale?' asked her father. I was stunned; she could hardly have driven quicker.

'Je vous attendais, au cas où vous ne pouviez pas garder ma vitesse!'

She was suggesting they might not be able to keep up! The chauffeur had filled up the Mercedes as well and smiled. It's not only the British that do jokes.

'Et je ne voulais pas faire peur à mon passager, pauvre garçon!' she went on.

I wasn't wild about being a 'pauvre garçon' who was likely to be scared.

After the tunnel we were in France and Dominique pointed out signs to lots of ski places I'd heard of like Chamonix. The scenery was fantastic and even better 'après nous avons quittés l'autoroute'. We came down to Lake Geneva, le lac Léman in French.

'I think in England you have a joke. In the car the children always ask "are we nearly there?" Yes?'

'Yes Richard and Sophie still do it, but mainly just to be annoying! Ennuyant? Is that right?'

'Non, on dit ennuyeux, I think ennuyant may be the old word. Mais maintenant je peux dire oui, nous y sommes presque. We are nearly there.'

We passed a side road with a baby sign and a green arrow, the word TENNIS and a picture of a little man with a racquet.

'Tu l'as vu, c'est notre club villageois. The courts are not bad. Il y en a trois courts, en toute saison, you say all-weather, pas comme Roland-Garros. Mais mon père, il a aussi son propre court, en gazon.'

'Je n'ai pas compris. Your father has his own court but gazon?'

'A grass court, comme Wimbledon.'

'Hey, ça sera magnifique!'

We turned into an impressive driveway and cruised in through large iron gates. I could see lawns running down to the lake. We pulled up outside the enormous front door with only a mild scrunch this time. I'd been keeping an eye on the Mercedes in the door mirror since we'd filled up and he'd always kept a sensible distance away but now glided in quietly behind.

People seemed to appear from everywhere. I wasn't sure what they all did, butlers or maids, cooks or house-keepers. My bag had been in the boot of the Peugeot (le coffre de la voiture ... or the trunk if you speak American) and I started to pull it out. Immediately Jean-Pierre came and grabbed it saying : 'If you please sir'. He wasn't in any sort of uniform ... and why did he speak to me in English? In fact they were all in ordinary summer clothes so there was no way to tell who might be a cook or a gardener.

Le Vicomte rushed over to help Dominique out of her car and arrived just too late. She ran to supervise Caroline's exit from the Mercedes but two of the staff were already holding an arm each.

'Merci, Jean-Pierre,' said le Vicomte to the driver. 'Tu sais quelle chambre Paul peut occuper.'

'Oui Papa.'

'Ouf,' I thought to myself, I could have really put my foot in it. It had already crossed my mind that you are supposed to give money to a porter! But Papa? Le Vicomte must be well over sixty and this guy looked as though he was hardly out of his teens.

'Jean-Pierre, il est comme un petit-fils adoptif. La dame qui aide Caroline est sa mère, et elle est ma cuisinière, chef de la cuisine. Ils sont venus de Syrie, il y a quelques années. Malheureusement, ils ne savent pas ce qui est arrivé à son mari, le père de Jean-Pierre. Tu as compris tout ça?'

'Oui … I think so. They arrived like refugees but without the father. But why does he call you Papa?'

'C'était une erreur. Quand il est arrivé, beaucoup plus jeune, il ne parlait presque aucun mot de français ou d'anglais. I said he could call me Grandpapa but he only understood Papa. It is very good because I like to confuse people.' He laughed loudly just as he had on the aircraft when we first met.

I thought that sounded a bit mean but decided I shouldn't say so, in English or French.

'Maintenant ça change. Je lui ai expliqué qu'il peut m'appeler Papa chez nous, mais à l'extérieur il doit faire preuve de respect. Mais il aime les blagues, you say jokes, comme moi. Récemment il a utilisé signor, monseigneur et autres choses comme ça. Le pire c'était 'Ja, mein Führer' avec un mouvement du bras droit. Heureusement nous étions seuls et je lui ai expliqué que ça c'était trop. Tu as compris?'

'Ouf, oui, mais c'est tout vrai? Je ne sais pas si vous … is this also a joke?'

'Non, pas du tout, c'est tout vrai! J'espère que peut-être vous deux deviendrez amis. Il joue également au tennis, mais pas au même niveau que toi.'

By now we had followed the others into the hall. Caroline had been whisked off to her room.

'Il faut manger, n'est-ce pas?' said her grandfather. 'It is very late but I have arranged for some lunch on the terrace. You will find us near the pool. I recommend you to wear a swimming costume.'

I love that expression. Dad has a joke about going to the sea when he was small. He says his grandmother had a hole in the elbow of her swimming costume. It was quite funny the first time but Dad does often repeat his jokes.

Jean-Pierre had come back and was asked to show me to my room. It was up two flights of stairs and through lots of passages. The place was so vast, I wasn't sure I'd find my way back. But a bouncy dog kept us company and seemed to be want to be friends with me.

'You prefer speak English,' he asked.

'Yes it's easier but I ought to keep trying French. You've learned both?'

He looked puzzled. 'Booth?'

Perhaps he didn't speak much English. 'Both … tous les deux.'

'Ah, mes excuses, j'ai pensé c'est une langue, anglais, français et booth!'

We laughed, both of us. He showed me from the window where the pool was. I could see a terrace and signs of lunch.

'Ça c'est Milou,' he said pointing at the dog. 'Vous avez lu les livres de Tintin? Milou était son chien, n'est-ce pas?'

This was confusing. Tintin's terrier, a fox terrier I think, was surely called Snowy. Then, hey, brainwave, Snowy would not have been his name in French.

'C'est bizarre parce-que c'est normalement un nom pour les filles, mais notre ami là est un chien, pas une chienne, comme le chien de Tintin.'

This was getting complicated but it could wait.

'Je vous laisse changer vos vêtements mais venez vite. Milou reste avec vous et il faut dire seulement "allez trouver Caroline!" '

'Hey, I think you should say "tu" to me.'

'OK, merci, nous allons nous tutoyer!'

'Et à Milou, il faut dire vous, pas tu?' I asked.

'Ouf, comme vous voulez, non, comme tu veux!'

We both laughed … funny language!

15 … FRIDAY LATER

The place was so vast, I'm not sure I would have found my way back but just whispering to Milou "allez trouver Caroline!" worked perfectly, although he had to stop and wait for me a couple of times. A late lunch had already been prepared on the terrace like a banquet. All the others were there ahead of me.

'Pas mal du tout là,' said Caroline. 'It's quite a nice place?'

'Fantastique, super,' I agreed. 'Tu viens ici ... often ... souvent?'

'Oui, presque toutes les vacances. En été, il fait si chaud à Paris, et notre appartement est si petit, nous venons pour plusieurs semaines. I am speaking much in French. You understand?'

'Yes, but it's bad for you,' I laughed. 'You have to practise your English.'

'But you understand what I say?'

'Oui, bien sûr. You come for holidays, particularly in summer because it's hot in Paris.'

'And ...'

'Your apartment is small.' We both laughed.

I suspected that her idea of a small apartment would be about the same as my idea of a big flat! And what we were eating would be her idea of un petit repas, a light lunch.

'Et mon grand-père, he permits me to invite my friends. Often I am here with many girl friends.'

'Perhaps, in the future, you may come again?' she suggested.

'Yes please, but there's no need to invite the other girls. One girl is enough.'

I'm sure I blushed, but she went red too.

'Il faut se baigner,' she said, as soon we'd finished lunch.

'Surely you can't swim, not yet,' I replied. I was pleased her grandfather had suggested I should wear swimming shorts; I certainly was not going to swim without them.

'Non, pas moi ... toi.'

'I'd rather stay with you; I can swim later.'

We walked down to the lake and found a bench to sit on. She sat down very carefully, it was clear that her back was still really painful. Milou came with us, he seemed to think it was his job to look after me.

'He's sweet,' I said, 'comme il est douce?'

'Oui, bon, mais comme il est mignon, c'est peut-être mieux. On dit mignon pour les enfants, les chiens et les chats.'

'Enfants de quel âge? Je suis mignon?'

She laughed. 'Bien sûr, of course you are very sweet!'

'OK, toi aussi,' I replied blushing, comme toujours.

I told her about the problem with the passports, how angry Joe had been and about his police escort with a baby Fiat.

'Et il revient quand?'

'Tomorrow, demain, Saturday, mais je ne sais pas à quelle heure.'

'Il aura laissé sa voiture à l'aéroport, n'est-ce pas?'

'Hey, come on, you are supposed to be talking English et moi français!'

'Ouf, OK, he leaves his car at the airport of Geneva?'

'Yes, oui.'

'To come here from the airport will take about one hour.'

Then I mentioned that I'd had to share a room with Luc. She looked straight at me.

'Pourquoi?' I explained that our rooms had already been taken by new people.

'Nos chambres étaient déjà ... on dit louées?'

'Yes, rented.'

'But it was OK; he wasn't as bad as I thought.'

'Quoi?'

'Well, he was moody and he cheats at tennis, but I know lots of boys who do that.'

'Moody, c'est quoi?'

'En français ... aucune idée, mais comme ça.' I made a gloomy face.

'De mauvaise humeur, yes, you say bad mood. And ... ?'

'And nothing.' I had decided not to tell her that Luc had caused the accident.

'Ma mère ... elle n'a dit rien quand on a proposé que tu dormes dans la même chambre?'

'Slowly ... your mother did what?'

'Who has proposed that you sleep in the room of Luc?'

'Claudia ... she knew there were two beds.'

'Mais oui, typique! Et ma mère ... my mother has said nothing?'

'Si, en fait, elle a dit que c'était pas nécessaire, je pourrais aller à l'autre hôtel avec ton grand-père.'

'Bon, mais tu n'as pas fait ça, pourquoi?'

'Joe thought it would be a waste of money, and I agreed. Mais Caroline, pourquoi tant de questions?'

'Parce que nous connaissons Luc très bien. Depuis plusieurs années'

'You've known him for years? How? Why?'

'My mother and the mother of Luc, they are old friends. Quand nous étions tout petits, nous allions à la même école, Luc et moi.'

'The same school? But I thought you said you hardly knew him?'

'Because I was angry, very angry, that he is here. Il a découvert que j'allais en Italie pour jouer au tennis, he has persuaded his mother that he must come, also that she must not tell my mother.'

'Why would he do that? He told me he'd got his father to agree, it was no problem because his father is very rich.'

'Quoi? Pas de problème pour son père? Oui, c'est vrai, pas de problème, pas du tout. Il n'en a pas, il n'a pas de père.'

'He has no father? Why would he lie about that?'

Caroline told me slowly the sad story. About four years ago, when Luc was just nine or ten, he'd heard his parents arguing one night. They had been having terrible rows for a long time. Luc knew that his father could be violent.

He got out of bed and went downstairs. His father threatened him too and his mother took him back to bed and stayed with him all night. The next day she took him away and they stayed with her mother.

'Je ne sais pas exactement ce qui arrivait après, mais on dit que Luc a décidé que le divorce était de sa faute. Tu as compris? He thought he was responsable.'

'Yes, his fault, so he was responsible.'

'But the most sad, he has need of a father. He hopes perhaps his father will return.'

'But he still sees his father, il y a du contact?'

'Almost never. He has had much help from a psychologue ou psychiatre, peut-être tous les deux … ouf … both!'

We laughed at her word 'both' but it was not a funny story.

'Alors, il me fait pitié mais je préfère l'éviter. Eviter, you say avoid him?'

'Yes. That's very sad, c'est triste mais on peut voir un peu du pére dans le fils? You can say that?'

'Oui, peut-être, mais assez, enough, we talk of something different.'

Of course, I thought, she still doesn't know that he'd caused her accident, but at least it had not been his plan to hurt her. And it shouldn't be necessary to tell her.

Milou was getting impatient with our talk. He went down close to the lake and came back carrying a stick. He dropped it at my feet.

'Il veut jouer avec toi,' said Caroline.

'No, I'm the one that speaks French ... il faut que tu parle anglais.'

'That's easy. He wishes to play with you.'

I stood up and threw the stick as far as I could.

'But no, he prefers to swim.'

'In the lake? ... mes excuses, dans le lac.'

'Mais oui.'

So when he brought the stick back, I threw it into the water but not too far. He looked at me as much as to say 'that's a bit pathetic', ran and dived full length almost landing on the stick. When he got back he rewarded me with a good wet shake.

'And you must swim,' she said. 'We go to the piscine.'

Milou started with us but quickly went back for his stick.

'He wishes to be your friend. It is necessary that you choose.'

'Ouf, il faut choisir,' I asked, 'choose what, quoi?'

'To be a friend of him or me?'

'Ouf, ça peut être difficile!'

She immediately looked hurt.

'Hey, joke! British humour, I don't how you say that in French.'

'A joke is une blague. On peut dire je rigole avec toi, I am joking. For humour we have the same word, mais British humour on ne peut pas traduire!' We both laughed.

By now we had arrived back at the terrace. Jean-Pierre was in the pool; Dominique and her father were sitting talking, still where we had had lunch.

'Joe has telephoned,' said Dominique. 'The funeral has finished and he will fly early tomorrow.'

I would have preferred him not to hurry but I didn't say so. I would probably have made a joke about it and probably been misunderstood.

'Alors, il va arriver demain à quelle heure?' I asked Dominique.

'Ça c'est bon, tu continues à parler français. Ton oncle est invité pour le déjeuner.'

There was a shout from the pool. As I turned Jean-Pierre threw a tennis ball towards me. Milou leapt but I managed to catch it and throw it back. He then threw it again tempting me to leap into the water but I was still wearing a shirt.

'Un petit moment,' I called. I had been wondering how to get into the pool, whether to try a showing-off dive or creep down the steps. He solved my problem by throwing the ball so that I had to jump for it. I made an enormous splash but arrived without the ball. Swimming almost next to me was Milou, ball in mouth and, if that's possible, a smug expression on his face.

The audience all clapped.

'OK,' I shouted to Caroline, 'I prefer to be your friend, je veux être ton ami!'

They all laughed although Dominique and her father cannot have understood the joke.

We then played a mean game of making Milou rush back and forth between us trying to get the ball but he seemed to enjoy it.

Meanwhile the others drifted away. I sat with Jean-Pierre by the pool for a while talking a mix of French and English. He told me a bit more of his story, a horrifying tale of how he had trekked with his mother from Syria through about seven or eight countries and how, by sheer luck, or the help of Allah as he put it, they had arrived in Evian, where the mineral water comes from, just along the lake from where we were sitting. His mother had tried to get work in a restaurant and the owner knew the Vicomte and knew that he was looking for a cook. Their real luck was that the Vicomte had all the necessary connections to get them papers to stay in France.

'Now I must aid my mother, to prepare the dinner. You are able to find your bedroom?'

'Yes, thanks, but I think my friend here will show me. Do you know what time dinner is?'

Jean-Pierre looked puzzled for a moment. 'Ah, the hour, l'heure pour dîner. I think twenty hours.' I could just about work out that would be eight o'clock.

Sensing activity, Milou was keen to help, wherever I was going. He led the way up a different staircase from the one I'd used before but straight to my room.

I had not really looked at it properly earlier when Jean-Pierre had shown me the way up. It was incredible. Double doors opened out onto a balcony with a view across the lake to Switzerland. I had my own bathroom, with an old-fashioned bath with feet. There was so much to sort out in my mind and the bath was the obvious place to do some thinking. I filled it almost to the brim.

'Poor Luc, poor boy,' I said to myself. I remembered lots of clues which hadn't registered at the time. He had been so upset by all our talk, by me getting angry. He'd asked if I was happy at home. I couldn't possibly have known about his problems or guessed why he was so mixed-up, but I still felt guilty at giving him a hard time.

My big worry now was Caroline's accident. Should I tell her that Luc had caused it? She might want to have him put away, permanently. He'd be sent to a mental home, for ever. But if I didn't tell her and she found out any way, she'd never trust me again. I wished Joe was here; he'd know what to do. But, when he arrived in the morning, it would be too late to talk to Caroline again.

'Merde,' I said to myself. 'La vie elle est très compliquée.' I giggled happily to myself; now I was even thinking in French!

Look at it from her point of view. She'd already had enough of him. She'd been upset by his stalking her, following her around.

Surely, aftcr all this, he'd give up, in which case, she needn't ever know.

'Right, that means don't tell her,' I said to myself.

I wanted to sort out in my mind what the writing business was all about. Joe had suggested it to me and it seemed that Grandpa had mentioned it to Caroline. And Joe had said that he didn't really know the Vicomte very well. But the bath water was getting cold. I climbed out and grabbed the towel; it was much bigger than me. I wrapped myself up and wandered out on to the balcony. The lights across the lake were stunning. I could hear conversation and laughter from the terrace below and I heard my name mentioned. I went back inside to find my watch.

'Merde, déjà vingt heures quinze!' I was late. I started to grab some clothes and, at that moment, the door was pushed open. It was my second-best friend, Milou. He'd been sent to find me.

Again he was the one to choose which staircase would be quickest.

'Ah, welcome,' smiled the Vicomte. 'Tu as dormi, peut-être? A snooze?'

'Non merci, j'ai pris un bain. C'était vraiment super. Et ... I had a lot to think about. How do you say that?'

Dominique helped : 'On peut réfléchir à quelque chose, ou bien réfléchir ... that would be good. Like reflect in English. Mais ... a lot to think about. Tell us!'

Caroline came immediately to my rescue.

'Maman, qu'est que c'est que ça pour une question? Tu ne peut pas faire ça. Pauvre garçon, il peut avoir des pensées, des réflexions privées, n'est-ce pas.'

I'm sure I went red but I was grateful to her, although I still wasn't keen to be un pauvre garçon.

'Il faut manger,' said Grandpa, but I mustn't start calling him that, even in my own head. But Jean-Pierre called him Papa so perhaps he wouldn't mind.

Jean-Pierre's mother not only cooked but served our supper to us.

'Fish from the lake,' said Caroline, 'it is a speciality, filets de perche.'

It was only a few hours since lunch, but a whole mass of little fillets were good and a mountain of chips, French fries, pommes frites were even better. I didn't say that it was the second time I'd had perch.

Only after the fish did it become clear why there were six chairs at the table apparently ready for more guests. Jean-Pierre and his mother came to join us for the dessert. I thought it was a super idea but guessed that not many owners of an enormous château would do that.

'Tiramisu,' said Caroline. Said in the French way it took me a moment to work out.

'Mais fait maison, how do you say that?'

'Made in the house?' I guessed.

'Exactly, but you'd say home-made, n'est-ce pas,' said Dominique.

'Exactly,' I repeated, 'and better, beaucoup mieux que le tiramisu du supermarché.'

Although I was sitting next to Caroline, we didn't get any chance to talk alone during the evening. In a way I was relieved; I still needed thinking time, on my own.

'Caroline, il est l'heure d'aller te coucher,' said Dominique. 'Tu as l'air bien fatiguée.' She did look tired. She still couldn't sit back in a chair or lie on her back.

'Oui,' she agreed, 'tu viens avec?' She kissed her grandfather and me good night and disappeared with Dominique. Le vicomte asked for some coffee on the terrace as Jean-Pierre and his mother started to clear things away from the table.

'Tu prends un café,' he asked me.

'Oui, s'il vous plaît.'

'Nous utilisons les capsules Nespresso. Alors il ya un grand choix, avec caféine, ou décafeiné, fort ou moins fort.'

'Ouf, I don't know, peut-être décafeiné, merci, although I shall not have a problem sleeping.'

It was still really warm out on the terrace.

'Alors, tu parles français beaucoup mieux maintenant,' said the Vicomte. 'You have learned much in a few days.'

'Merci,' I replied. 'C'est bon que j'ai rencontré ta ... ta ... granddaughter, et mes excuses, j'ai dit ta, il faut dire votre!'

'Don't worry, that's not a problem. For granddaughter on dit petite-fille. A daughter, she is une fille, a granddaughter une petite-fille. Et maintenant tu prends un petit cognac?'

'Merci, non merci. Pas de cognac, même un petit cognac!'

I'd already had plenty of wine with dinner; I didn't need brandy too. If Mum worried about Uncle Joe being a bad influence, what would she think of this guy?

When Dominique came back, I said I was ready for bed, thanked them both and kissed her good-night, on both cheeks of course, but I thought one each side was probably enough. Jean-Pierre and his mother had already said good night and Milou had gone with them. I left Caroline's Mum and Grandpa together.

16 ... SATURDAY

In bed I started thinking about the future. Would I see Caroline again? How, where, when? Luc and I had exchanged addresses; would I hear from him again? Eventually I fell asleep.

I had got in the habit of a morning swim in Italy. Why not here too? I looked down from the balcony. I could hear splashing noises from the pool but I couldn't see who was there. It could be Jean-Pierre, probably not Dominique and certainly not Caroline; she would not be able to use the pool for quite a while.

As I went downstairs I worried again about French naturisme. I started to tip-toe. If someone there was swimming naturiste, I'd slink back upstairs without them seeing me. I crept out on to the terrace. As I rounded the corner towards the pool, I stuck close to the wall, and bumped straight into the Vicomte, coming the other way. He had bare feet, which was why I'd heard nothing.

'Bonjour,' he grunted. I'd literally knocked the wind out of him.

'Bonjour et excusez-moi. I was trying to be quiet. I didn't know if you were all still asleep,' I lied quickly.

'Pas de problème, tu vas te baigner? Il fait assez froid là, nous n'avons pas de chauffage pour la piscine. Tu comprends?'

'Oui merci. You said you don't have heating for the pool. It was the same at the hotel in Italy but I swam every morning. It wakes you up.'

'Oui moi aussi. Alors, have a good swim. See you at breakfast.'

As he walked away, his bathing robe swung wide open but, from behind, I still couldn't be sure if he was a naturiste!

We all had breakfast together. Caroline was much better.

'Et tu as bien dormi?' I asked.

'Yes, thank you. I have slept very well. For the first time I could lie sometimes on my back.'

'Super, ça va mieux, alors.'

By now I was desperate to have some time alone with her, particularly to discuss the writing idea. But the Vicomte insisted on giving me a game of tennis. The château had its own brilliant grass court as well as the pool. I was a bit nervous that he might have a heart attack or something; he must be well over sixty, probably seventy.

'Eh bien,' he said after we'd hit a few balls, 'tu peux commencer.' He banged the spare balls down to my my end. Milou had come to join us and wanted to act as a ball-boy but was told to sit. He watched patiently.

Playing on grass makes a big difference; the ball comes through much faster. I served quite gently and won the first game to fifteen. We changed ends. His first serve was a cracking ace straight down the middle. He won that game without me getting a single point.

'Tu peux servir un peu plus fort si tu veux, pas si doucement,' he laughed. He wanted me to serve harder!

For the next hour I had to play out of my skin, and took the set 7-5. Even then, I wasn't sure if maybe he'd let me win. It turned out that he had been a Davis Cup player long ago; he was the one who'd encouraged Caroline originally and coached her when she was small.

'Why didn't you tell me?' I asked Caroline afterwards.

'Quoi?'

'Tu n'as pas dit que ton grand-père ... is an expert.'

'Oui, il est assez expérimenté,' she replied, 'he has good experience!'

'You can say that again!'

'Quoi?'

'Rien,' I laughed.

Joe soon turned up in George, the Discovery. He'd come straight from the airport in Geneva, so he hadn't changed. He was wearing a dark suit, very smart. Of course, with all the other developments, I'd quite forgotten about the funeral.

'You look a bit different,' I said, 'I'm not used to seeing you dressed for business, très élégant.'

'Well it made sense to go dressed for the funeral and I didn't have time to think about other kit.'

'How was it? Did many people go?' I asked him.

'No, just a handful. Some of the residents and staff from the apartment house where Gran lived and a few old friends.'

'And then you had to stand around for ages by the grave. That must have been depressing.'

'No, Paul, Gran was cremated.'

I hadn't ever thought about it before. I suppose cremation's a good idea; by then you don't know that much about it. What a choice, worms or flames? But I didn't say that to Uncle Joe.

We were going to have a quick lunch on the terrace and then Joe and I had to leave. The morning had gone and I'd had no chance to talk to Caroline alone.

When it came to the coffee stage, I suggested to Caroline that I'd like to have a last look at the lake. I managed it without blushing.

'Oui, bonne idée,' she agreed.

We could only talk for a few minutes. There was no need to talk about Luc again, which was a relief.

'J'espère que ... no, dammit, I'm going to speak English.'

I grabbed her hand.

'I hope very much we shall meet again. You said maybe I can come here and you must come to London.'

'Oui, bien sûr. Ça me plairait. Et si tu viens en hiver, on peut faire du ski. Tu as fait ça déjà?'

'Only once when I was about eight ... it was brilliant. And snow-boarding, that looks great.'

'OK,' she said, 'we can make big plans. Et il faut me donner ton adresse courriel, email.'

Of course neither of us had anything to write with and I didn't have my phone either.

'Mais, ce n'est pas nécessaire, Joe a déjà demandé à ma mère notre adresse à Paris!'

I laughed. 'Brilliant, super, formidable.

'Et j'espère que tu peux vite recommencer à jouer tennis, peut-être avec ton grand-père.'

'Yes, les blessures, my wounds are already better. I could play now but without shirt.'

I don't know how my face looked but she roared with laughter. I took the opportunity to kiss her goodbye but only quickly in case anyone was looking; we walked back up the lawn.

After lots of goodbyes, thank-yous and more kissing, we were on our way. Almost immediately I realised that I hadn't quizzed Caroline about the writing idea.

We had to drive back through the city of Geneva and Joe pointed out the famous fountain. It's an amazing jet of water that comes straight up out of the lake and climbs high into the sky.

'Je vais t'accompagner au retour à Londres.'

'Hey, did I hear right? You're coming with me?'

This was good news; I wouldn't have to have the dreaded label round my neck.

'Oui, il faut que j'aide ton papa après la mort de notre maman, le testament etc. Il faut vider son appartement et donner les instructions pour la vente.'

'Vider means empty, like clear everything, and vente is sale?'

'How's Stumpy?' I asked him, once we were on the Swiss autoroute.

'I've no idea. You're forgetting, I only had a few hours at home, my home, to unload stuff and I left again before six a.m., to fly to London.'

'Yea, of course. Stupid me.'

He wanted to know what else had happened in Italy.

I told him the whole saga, of the row with Luc and how he'd owned up, how he'd been scared I would hurt him, and then what Caroline had told me afterwards, of Luc's history.

'C'est la vie, that's life. It was only because of the farce with the passports that we had to go back. If that hadn't happened, you might have decided by now that it was Claudia all the time! But, the thing is, we wouldn't have known.'

'But it doesn't make much sense, none at all. Luc's got enough bloody problems without creating new ones. Why would he do that? Just plain stupidity? Jealousy of me?'

'Paul, we can't know. I told you before ... things happen sometimes and we never know why. Let's talk about something else.'

'I don't know how to put this, Joe, but you haven't been quite straight with me, a few times.'

'Ouf, you should try to put that in French but that would be a bit tough. You mean about when Grandma died.'

'OK, j'essaie en français. Pas ça, pas grand-mère. Tu as dit que tu ne connait pas le Vicomte, ou pas bien. Et il ya l'idée, about writing, l'idée d'écriture. Caroline's Grandpa had put the same idea to her!'

'Yes, sorry, let me come clean. It started when I was a journalist long ago, first with the Financial Times and then the Economist. I wrote a piece for the Economist about hidden wealth, how some great riches are tucked away in anonymous accounts in the name of not very respectable lawyers. It interested the Vicomte and he wanted to speak to me. Most people write anonymously for the Economist but he managed to track me down and asked for my help.

'He is, or maybe was by now, a director of one of the very old private banks in Geneva. There are several of them, very old and very respectable, although they may have some not very nice clients. Dictators and tyrants are always rumoured to have Swiss bank accounts.

They had a client which was a charity with lots and lots of money, very big money. It was doing fantasticly good works but nobody knew where it's money came from. Drug dealers in South America, gun-runners in the Middle East, you guess.'

'Ouf, how can I?'

'No, I didn't mean that you have to! But you get the picture. And so I had to do some detective work but the big absolutely overriding condition was secrecy. And I must only write up the story with his approval.'

'And you were successful?'

He put his finger to his lips … 'nous sommes toujours de très bons amis, c'est tout ce que je peux dire!'

'Bloody hell. Sorry, but that story calls for bad language.'

'And what about the writing and, before that, how come we were on the aircraft together?'

'Let me get us some food and then we can go on talking.'

'Alors, qu'est-ce que nous mangeons ce soir?'

'Bon, un menu paysan mais italien … on commence avec une salade verte, roquette ou rucola, arrosée d'huile d'olive et de vinaigre balsamique … il faut traduire?'

'Non merci, j'ai compris, a bit of greenery sprayed with oil and vinegar … et puis?'

'Pasta, tagliatelles alla pesto genovese!'

'OK, pesto's green so that'll be long white thong things with green sauce?'

'Thanks for the flattery!'

I know that Uncle Joe's a pretty good cook but it had been a long day for him. He'd only come back from London this morning.

'Je peux t'aider?'

'Oui, il y a quelque chose de très important à faire. Le moulin à poivre est vide. Dans l'armoire là il y a une boîte de poivre noir.'

I hesitated.   Vide is empty, poivre is pepper, armoire is a cupboard. And I even knew that a moulin is a windmill.

'Your windmill is empty,' I laughed, but before he could correct me I grabbed the pepper-mill and opened the cupboard.

'Pas de problème!'

'Et là, au coin,' he pointed at a wine rack in the corner of the kitchen, 'une bouteille de Beaujolais Villages, s'il te plaît. C'est fait avec les raisins Gamay, comme les vins suisses mais c'est moins cher.'

I even managed to find a corkscrew.

'And food will be ready soon so you can go and se laver les mains si tu veux.'

Of course I was able to use the same bedroom with its own bathroom.   Joe hadn't bothered to change towels or anything as he had expected me to come back from Italy with him before all the complications of him having to fly backwards and forwards.

I waited until after the greenery salad before I started my questions. With the pasta he'd made an extra salad of red onions and tomato.

'That's really good,' I said. 'It's a bit sweet.'

'Well spotted, still oil and vinegar, but tomatoes need salt, whatever the health merchants say, and then a good sprinkle of sugar.'

'Ouf, alors, arrosé de sucre,' I laughed.

'Please tell me in English where the writing idea comes from.'

It took a while but he explained that he had mentioned to Grandpa that he was taking me to Italy for tennis and that that fitted Grandpa's writing scheme for which he already had Caroline in mind. She was also a good tennis player so it would be fixed for us to meet but first he wanted to meet me to check that I was the right candidate for the scheme.

'So he flew to London specially to fly back with me, I can't believe it!'

'No, he flies to London at least once a month, so he just had to adjust his programme a bit.'

'And fix the airline!'

'Pas de problème, c'est un bon client, n'est-ce pas? They wanted to upgrade you to business class but he refused. That might have made you more suspicious sooner!'

'Merde, ce n'est pas juste! Unfair! But what's the scheme?'

'I think it's a great idea. A bilingual novel, English boy meets French girl and they teach each other. But I should say two novels because they both write. Le vicomte is passionate about getting young people to communicate across borders. He's already supported lots of different efforts and you know what he's done for Jean-Pierre and his Mum.'

'Joe, no way, that's far too ambitious for me. I struggle to write two pages of anything!'

'Je suis certain que Caroline n'a dit presque rien à toi à ce sujet.'

'That's true but mainly because we ran out of time.'

'Le grand-père, il croit que tu peux le faire, moi aussi je pense que tu peux le faire et, le plus important, Caroline elle pense que tu peux le faire. Everybody thinks you can do it!'

'Merde, no, it's too important for me to tackle, too big, shit! How would we work together?'

'Sorry, you don't need to, you just have to meet occasionally to compare notes, but probably not until you've got a first full draft!'

I really did not know what to think.

'Joe, you must be dead, after such a long day. I'm happy to go to bed and have another string of questions for you tomorrow.'

'Mais en français!'

'What's the plan for tomorrow, it's my last day.'

'Well you could choose between my lap-top or my iMac and start work, straight away! But I have fixed for us to play some doubles up at La Veyre, if you don't mind.'

'Joe, great, thanks. Merci infiniment!'

'Non, de rien.'

I got ready slowly for bed, still churning so many things over in my mind. If I went along with this crazy writing idea, it would mean continuing contact with Caroline. And it looked as though I didn't really have any option any way. I lay awake for what seemed ages but must finally have dozed off.

17 ... SUNDAY

'This weather's annoying,' said Joe as he was making cups of tea for us. 'Il fait si beau qu'il faut jouer à l'extérieur.'

'What do you mean? It's a perfect day, don't you like playing outdoors?'

'No,' he replied, 'I just find it so much easier to play on the indoor courts, but I know we can't. The others wouldn't agree. Outdoors you get sun in your eyes, sand in your shoes and I'll probably get burned.'

'Ouf, mon pauvre oncle!'

I'm sure he wanted to ask if I was already working out ideas for my book but he was kind enough not to.

He had pains au chocolat again for us for breakfast but I decided to be really grown-up and share his coffee. That meant we didn't have the capsule type. He used a thing called Moka Express which heats up on top of the stove and makes the most grown-up coffee you could imagine.

'Ouf, ça c'est incroyable!'

'Oui, cela va mettre les poils sur la poitrine,' he said. 'Compris?'

'No, sorry, that will put something on something?'

'Hairs on your chest,' he laughed. 'Tu as encore des vêtements pour le tennis? C'est pas nécessaire de porter du blanc.'

I'd already thought about kit.

'Oui j'ai lavé des chemises dans la douche, merci. And that reminds me … je n'ai pas pris une douche ce matin. Je peux aller faire ça et puis m'habiller pour notre match.'

He was still reading his week-end FT and just waved agreement.

'Mais,' he shouted as I walked away. 'il faut apporter quelques autres vêtements parce que nous pourrions rester et déjeuner avec mes amis au club.'

'D'accord, mon oncle.'

It was no distance up the hill from Vevey, almost to the autoroute. We turned off just by the Modern Times Hotel. Apparently it's named after a film by Charlie Chaplin; he lived near there and there's a super museum about his work.

'Hey, Joe, look, there's one of the helicopters you told me about.'

He'd explained that the restaurant at the tennis club has a good reputation and some of the working helicopter people often drop in for lunch, literally!

'Il est un peu tôt pour le déjeuner, non? He is here for a late breakfast?'

He didn't answer but turned off down the side road towards the machine.

'Quoi? What are you doing?'

As he pulled to the side of the road someone jumped out of the pilot's seat, down on to the grass, and walked towards us.

'Monsieur Domingo, bonjour. Exactement à l'heure, comme attendu. Il fait beau pour un vol.'

He turned to me.

'Good morning sir, it is a fine day for flying.' His English accent was almost too good to be true. 'May I just see your passport please.'

I couldn't quickly remember where I'd last put it but not in my tennis bag. Before I could say anything Joe waved two passports.

'Je les ai gardés hier après notre retour.' He grinned.

'But where are we going …? And why are you Domingo? He's a singer isn't he, opera,' I whispered.

'As to where we're going you only need surely un seul conjecture, n'est-ce pas?…'

145

'Hang on, un seul conjecture, that must be one guess, just one guess?'

'Exactement!'

'Ouf, mille fois ouf, même infiniment ouf, but why, for tennis?'

'Oui, bien sûr.   Monsieur le grand-père était en colère, très fâché que tu aies gagné hier. Il veut se venger.'

'Fâché means angry, yes, and the rest?'

'En colère is just another way of saying angry and se venger you should guess, revenge.'

'But you wanted to play, didn't you?'

'Mm, I shall, it will be doubles but I doubt that your girl-friend can play.'

I scowled at him; he knew I didn't like that expression.

'And the surname, ton nom de famille, Domingo?'

'J'expliquerai plus tard, later.'

By now we had tennis bags out of the car and the pilot had loaded them into a small hold behind the seats.

'This is an Airbus Twin Squirrel, AS 355,' he said to me, 'un Ecureil 2. You have flown in one before?'

'No, never, not any sort of helicopter.'

We were helped up into the seats behind him and only now I noticed a small boy sitting next to him.   He turned and introduced the boy.

'Mon co-pilote aujourd'hui, c'est Antoine, mon fils.'

Antoine said 'bonjour' and we shook hands.

'Et votre fils a combien d'années?' asked Joe.

'Il a neuf ans mais il est déjà bien expérimenté.'

The pilot turned to me and laughed.   'My son is nine but he is very experienced.'

I looked at Joe but decided I couldn't ask : 'is he really going to fly us?' The whole trip was exciting enough. I decided I'd rather be flown by Batman than Robin.

I still wanted to know what the trip was all about and why Domingo but I was handed a pair of headphones and from then on we couldn't really talk. It was great to listen in to the air traffic messages.

Way back at the beginning I said that I liked the takeoff from Heathrow airport. This was a whole different experience, an almost vertical climb, a swing towards the south and ... is my stomach still with me?

We flew over the enormous HQ building of Nestlé which Joe had pointed out earlier. I could see lots of people in the big swimming pool next door to it, many of them shading their eyes as they looked up at us. Then immediately we were out over the lake. As we climbed, more mountains came into view and the pilot talking to us over the headphones pointed out Mont Blanc.

'Ah oui oui oui,' I was able to say, 'mais c'est pas le montagne le plus haut en Europe!'

The others all laughed.

There were control messages as we crossed from Switzerland into France and, just very few minutes later, I could spot the château and we were on our way down. I suddenly realised that the pilot had both hands in his lap. Antoine was actually in control but probably only for a few moments.

The family were outside waiting. I could see Caroline holding Milou on a short lead as he was leaping up and down. The pilot took us gently down to the smoothest possible landing on the grass between the house and the lake.

We jumped out and did that bit of walking away almost bent double to avoid the still whirling blades, just like you see on television!

'Bonjour! Prêt pour cette petite Davis Cup?' asked Grandpa as he greeted us. 'Angleterre contre France/Syrie.'

That answers one question, I thought. I couldn't believe that Caroline would be allowed to play. Syria must mean Jean-Pierre would partner the old man.

I kissed Caroline and her Mum and Joe and I were sent to get ready for the big match. We put our bags in what had been my bedroom and Joe burst open two new tubes of balls.

'I have so many questions all the time,' I said to him. 'Please explain why the pilot called you Domingo.'

'Oh that's another hangover from my original work with le vicomte. I told you it was all very confidential and he suggested a way of leaving messages for each other which only we would understand. Of course this was before mobile phones were around.'

'How did it work?'

'Ça reste secret,' he said but laughing. 'On utilise le jour de la semaine avec un changement de langue. Aujourd'hui c'est dimanche. Il pouvait dire au pilote qu'il va chercher Monsieur Sunday or Monsieur Dimanche mais il a choisi Monsieur Domingo, Sunday in Spanish, which sounds more convincing, doesn't it?'

I thought for a moment. 'But the pilot looked at our passports, why didn't he say anything?'

'He must be in on the game. Grandpa only keeps it going now for fun. I've told you that he likes to confuse people. He probably told the pilot a string of lies that I'm a celebrity or something. And it ties in with his enthusiasm for multi-lingual chat!'

'That's all good fun but I find it a bit scary if you sometimes won't know if he's joking or not.'

We went to find the others out on the terrace. They were all coming to watch, even Jean-Pierre's mother, to support the Syrian half of their team.

The whole match was played for fun. Yesterday we had played with good tennis balls but this time Grandpa produced a bag of balls of all sorts. Joe started looking through them.

'As I had expected, a mélange, a mixture, good ones for you to serve, rubbish for us? J'ai un cadeau pour toi et tu es obligé d'accepter.'

He produced the tubes he'd opened upstairs.

Grandpa stayed mainly at the net often going to play the ball then leaving it at the last moment for Jean-Pierre to scream around behind him. He, Grandpa, also kept calling out the score in more languanges than I'd ever heard. And that reminded me.

When we changed ends there was a pause for water.

'Minä rakastan sinua,' I said to Grandpa.

'Ho, ho,' he laughed loudly. 'This boy has a good memory. From my notebook, yes? But you cannot say it to me. Perhaps to Caroline?' … and he laughed again.

The others were sitting near enough to hear him.

'Quoi?' shouted Caroline. 'You speak about me.'

Grandpa repeated what I'd said and what he'd said. Dominique laughed; she clearly knew what it means. She whispered to Caroline.

'OMG,' laughed Caroline, 'mais il a dit ça à grand-père.'

'Oui, mais sans savoir une traduction. I think he still doesn't know.'

'I love you,' shouted Dominique at me.

There was turmoil, everybody talking to each other, Dominique explaining to Jean-Pierre so that he could explain to his Mum. I had to remind Joe that I'd looked at the notebook on the flight out.

'That comes from about sixty years ago. When I was at school, I had a friend and we were both already enthusiasts for foreign languages. We did research for "I love you" in all languages, to be prepared for meeting girls!' Grandpa was laughing happily. 'It was difficult before Google had been invented.'

'Déjà vilain comme garçon,' said Dominique, 'a naughty boy.'

The score was not important and when we got to six games all, we played a tie-break … we let them win it!

I sat next to Caroline at lunch.

'Tu as commencé, le roman bilingue?' I asked.

'Oui, et non. Mon grand-père m'a donné un petit cahier comme le sien ...'

'Mes excuses, il faut que tu parle anglais.'

'Merde, or I can say shit? My grandfather has given me a book, the same like his. I commence only to make some notes. And he has said to me : ne pas essayer de démarrer au début, do not commence at the commencement! Merde, that's bad English.'

'He means don't start at the beginning. Joe m'a dit la même chose. And please don't say shit. I cannot explain, I think merde is OK but if you say shit, it sounds awful, affreux n'est-ce pas.'

'Ouf, comme tu es mignon.'

Yes, of course, I went red, again.

It was not so long after lunch that we all heard the rattle of the helicopter returning. Caroline and I had agreed that we could talk to each other from time to time, by phone or Skype and we'd compared notes about the different messaging web-sites. But we'd also agreed that we needed to make plenty of progress before we exchanged some chapters. It was really only now that I recognised that I seemed to be committed to the project.

Lots of farewells all over again and this time I didn't feel so embarrassed about giving Caroline a special kiss goodbye. I just whispered 'minä rakastan sinua' but I laughed a bit in case she thought I was being too serious! She laughed too.

At the very last moment just as I was about to climb back in to the helicopter Grandpa gave me a note-book, just like his. I started to flick through and spotted a few hieroglyphics here and there. No doubt I would struggle to interpret and/or get the jokes.

'Merci, Monsieur, merci beaucoup!'

'Ah mais non, pas Monsieur, pourquoi pas Grand-papa?'

'Ouf, OK, d'accord, merci Grand-papa!'

Now I was really one of the family. But had he guessed that I was already referring to him as Grandpa? It was a bit scary, again.

The flight was even better this time because the sun was much lower in the sky, silhouetting some of the mountains. We still couldn't really talk but Joe mouthed the name of the mountains at the far end of the lake, les Dents du Midi, totally spectacular.

At Joe's home he wanted me to start working on one of his Macs.

'No, I'd rather start to scribble some notes in my new little book. Un peu de préparation, n'est-ce pas.'

'Avant ton chef d'œuvre!'

'Aucune idée, what's that mean?'

'We use it in English, well some people do, it means your masterpiece.'

'Ah, good, but I doubt I shall write a chef d'oeuvre until I'm your age, and that's a very long way off!'

We had a quiet evening and I did manage to get some notes on paper but I spent most of the time thinking about my new second family. It was a bit tough that I now had quite a task to live up to their expectations.

18 ... MONDAY

The following morning, Mum and Dad were at Heathrow to meet us.

'Didn't the other two want to come and meet their big brother?' I asked.

'Yes dear, of course they did, but we told them they couldn't, because it would have been a bit of a crowd with Joe and all your luggage,' Mum replied.

'Well, sorry I came,' laughed Joe.

'Now you know that's not what I meant, Joe.' She turned to me. 'Richard and Sophie will want to hear all your news when we get home.'

'And Ben, he's all right? I want to tell him all about Saint Bernards. I would have bought him one of those barrels to go round his neck, but we never finally got to see them.'

We all piled into the car and Dad hit the M4.

'I want to hear about your girl friend,' he said. He's really subtle, my Dad.

'She's just a friend, Dad. And any way she's spent most of the last few days lying flat on her tummy, so we didn't have much chance to get to know each other.'

Joe gurgled a laugh, which Mum and Dad ignored.

'And what about the French boy?' asked Mum. 'You said you were going to smash him or have a fight with him or something. I'm sure he wasn't as unpleasant as you thought, dear. I hope you weren't unkind.'

'No, Mum, I wasn't unkind to him, I promise. In fact Luc turned out to be OK and we hope to play each other one day at Wimbledon!'

'Et si vous continuez, tous les deux, à poser des questions difficiles, je ne parle que français,' I laughed.

'Aucun problème!' said Mum. I'd forgotten that she does speak some French.

At home Richard and Sophie wanted to know all about everything but it was clear that most of their talk must have been about Caroline. I suppose that's not so surprising with the accident and so on. Ben was as excited as ever to see me and he doesn't ask difficult questions. I'd tell him all about St Bernards later.

Joe sat down at the table with Dad, who'd already prepared a lot of paper-work. I guess it was connected with Gran's will and things. I wondered if perhaps she might have left some money to her grand-children. It would be good if I could buy a new Mac like Joe's, much easier to work on than my old Dell machine.

I ran upstairs, threw my bag on my bed and said hello to my old panda. He asked me if I'd had a good time. Then I spotted a parcel on the table, wrapped for transport like an Amazon parcel, but not from them. It had Swiss International labels on it. Had I left something behind? Not possible, it couldn't have got here ahead of us. I ripped it open … a new MacBook, incredibly thin and quite beautiful.

'What the hell?' I said to myself (or something similar).

I tore open an envelope.

'Meilleures salutations … ton nouveau grand-père! Et bonne chance avec l'écriture!'

I rushed back downstairs like a mad thing and showed everybody.

'Wow!' was the universal reaction.

Then, quick as a flash, Richard said : 'You won't need your old Dell any more, will you, Paul? You'd probably like to give it to your favourite brother.'

He's a bright boy. Sophie kindly decided not to put in a bid herself.

'When did this arrive?' I asked.

'Quite a few days ago,' said Mum.

'But ..., mais, c'est pas possible ...!'

I looked at Joe who was grinning happily.

'You two old ... I don't know what to call you ... fixers? The whole thing was planned in advance. I can't ever trust you again. Unless ...'

Mum was about to tell me not to be rude but I quickly said :

'Unless you fix that trip to Monte Carlo ... with the girls!'

Now they all looked confused so I ran back up to my room.

I was soon at the table, new machine plugged in.

'C'est mieux de ne pas commencer au commencement,' Grandpa had said and Joe had said something similar.

'Don't try and start at the beginning, mais pourquoi pas?' I asked myself. Joe had told me that he writes very fast but always spends ages editing, trying to improve his first go.

'Si ça ne marche pas, je peux toujours le changer. Like Joe, I should get some words down first and then edit it.

'Alors, il faut commencer où? Where do I begin? A l'aéroport de Heathrow peut-être?'

"Just imagine ... I had to walk through the departure lounge at Heathrow Airport with a large wallet thing hanging round my neck. I was following two tiny children, both wearing labels like me. It was totally humiliating.

It was my first proper trip away on my own and we'd had a real row ..."

*** FIN ***

46071447R10094

Printed in Poland
by Amazon Fulfillment
Poland Sp. z o.o., Wrocław